GW00503002

The *Mary Fletcher*

EXETER MARITIME STUDIES

General Editor: Stephen Fisher

Also by Edmund Eglinton
The Last of the Sailing Coasters (1982)

Exeter Maritime Studies
No. 5

The *Mary Fletcher*

Seven Days in the Life of a Westcountry Coasting Ketch

by

Edmund Eglinton

Edited and introduced by Basil Greenhill
with notes and charts by Peter Allington

University of Exeter Press

First published in 1990 by
University of Exeter Press
Reed Hall
Streatham Drive
Exeter EX4 4QR
United Kingdom

British Library Cataloguing in Publication Data
Eglington, Edmund *1902–*
    The Mary Fletcher : seven days in the life of a west country coasting ketch. –
(Exeter maritime studies, No. 5).
    1. Bristol Channel. Freight transport. Shipping. Cargo ships : Sailing coasters, history - Biographies
    I. Title II. Greenhill, Basil *1920– III.* Allington, Peter IV. Series
387.5092

ISBN 0-85989-326-X

Printed in the UK by BPCC Wheatons Ltd, Exeter

CONTENTS

INTRODUCTION

The wooden merchant sailing ship was one of Western European mankind's most important tools from the twelfth century to the early twentieth century, and until the last 60 years or so of her era, she was the predominant means of sea transport. Now not only has she ceased to exist, but her world is one we have lost, together with many other 'worlds'—systems of human living which grew out of the necessities of earlier circumstances.

It may not be widely appreciated today that until the First World War, the small wooden sailing vessel, 40 to 120 or so feet long, at the largest, and broad and deep in proportion, schooner, or, more and more as time went on, ketch rigged, still played an important part in the economy of the haven communities of south west England. There were hundreds of these vessels, many of them owned by small shareholding groups of local people, merchants, shipbuilders, shopkeepers, farmers, lawyers, doctors, quarrymen, brickmakers, widows, shipmasters, schoolteaches, brokers. One of their number was usually designated as the 'managing owner' and formally registered as such on the ship's documentation, and the Master was usually a shareholder and played an important part in the successful, or otherwise, operation of the vessel. This kind of relatively high-risk venture with small individual investment was known in Sweden and in the Swedish-speaking parts of the great archipelagoes of Finland, where the greater part of the investment came from the agrarian community, as *almogeseglation*, 'peasant seafaring', and that, if we are not too particular about the definition of the term peasant, is not a bad name for it. But it must be realised that for some communities, Appledore in North Devon is a prime example in the south west of England but there are plenty of others elsewhere in Britain and Europe, virtually the whole economy of the community was based on the carrying trade, the movement of other people's cargoes in small quantities between other ports and shipping places in wooden sailing vessels.

These wooden sailing vessels continued to be built in small numbers until the fateful year of 1914. Even in the 1920s there was still plenty of work for a well managed vessel with a vigorous and very hardworking Master. The cargo book of the Plymouth-built, Appledore-owned, Barnstaple-registered, ketch *Haldon* from 1923–24, the two years immediately before that in which the imaginary ketch *Mary Fletcher* made the passages described in this book, shows continuous employment. Between September 1922 and November 1924, the *Haldon* loaded and discharged cargoes in London, Lydney, Gweek, Plymouth, Llanelly, Courtmacsherry, Ballycotton, Truro, Penarth, Avonmouth, Bridgwater, Looe, Newport, Clonakilty, Port Talbot, Mevagissey, Gloucester, Liverpool, Antwerp, Topsham, Bideford, Barnstaple, Bristol, Skibbereen, Glasgow, Newross and Kinsale.

But it was a very hard life. In the early 1970s the Master of the *Haldon* in those two years of 1922–24 (who was successful enough to be able to sell his vessel and retire in comfort at the age of 50) Captain W. J. Slade of Bideford, wrote in his book, *Westcountry Coasting Ketches* (1974):

> For most of the time I was at sea we were living sordid lives, earning very little money for endless hard grinding work and, in retrospect, I can see we were often in physical danger. The so-called good old days at sea were anything but good in modern times. We were among the least regarded members of society, skilled manual workers, but largely cut off from the comprehension of those of our contemporaries not directly connected with the sea. We were a neglected sub-branch of the complex family tree of the working class before the first World War. When we stepped aboard our vessels from the shore we moved from the early 20th century to the late 18th.

Life in these vessels has been described in general terms in a number of books, notably in Captain Slade's own autobiographical classic *Out of Appledore* (1980). In *The Merchant Schooners* (1988), I attempted something of a portrait of this particular part of the carrying trade at sea between 1870 and 1940. In Edmund Eglinton's other book, *The Last of the Sailing Coasters* (1982), he vividly described the differences between sailing the wooden commercial sailing vessel of the early years of this century and modern yachting:

> More than half a century later than the passage described one has got used to seeing, on the medium of television, young people of both sexes sail single-handed across the Atlantic in modern fibreglass yachts with light man-made fibre sails, and every conceivable navigational appliance—the modern ratchet winches for winding in the sheets within arm's length of the person in the cockpit, jib headed mainsails and mizzens, the luffs of which run up, and down, in grooves on the aft sides of the masts, self-steering gear that allows the vessel to be left to sail on her own for hours, or even days, while the crew sleeps, or attends to the many chores that always demand attention. Our efforts in the *Garlandstone* may not seem worthy of recording. But actually there is no comparison. The *Garlandstone* (as were all the other 'vessels') was built as ships were a century before her time—except that she was more shapely. Her frame would have been 7″ or 8″ square oak placed only a few inches apart, covered outside with planking from 3″ to 2½″ in thickness, and planked inside with 3″ pitch pine, making her sides over a foot in thickness, but her bottom was made up of stouter timbers and was probably 14–15 inches thick. Her deck beams would have been 8″ square oak and the deck planking 2½″ thick. Built to take the ground when loaded with 120 tons of coal, these massive timbers were more than necessary, but the weight was tremendous.
> This heavy structure needed very heavy gear to drive it along. Her mainmast from keelson to head would have been nearly 60 feet in length, 14–15″ in diameter at deck level and about nine inches at the head. The timber alone (pitch pine) in this mast weighed well over a ton. Her

topmast would have been 30 feet in length tapering from seven or eight inches to about four inches at the truck. The mizzen mast would have been about 60 feet long and 10 inches in diameter at the base to five inches at the truck, with booms and gaffs for each mast in proportion. The bowsprit would have been around 28 to 30 feet long and 10 inches in diameter. Her main and mizzen rigging was set up with hempen lanyards rove through dead-eyes as in Nelson's day. Her main halyards were of four inch manilla, likewise the standing jib sheets; there were two other jibs. Except for her wire shrouds, her rig and all her gear was very little different to any fore and aft rig that sailed the seas at the time of Trafalgar.

The foregoing may be taken as a fairly close description of the *Mary Fletcher* herself.

Despite all that has been published there is on record no detailed account of the actual handling of these vessels, hour by hour, day by day, of the routine of life on board, and of the way the Master, the mate, and such hands as there may have been worked together. After the publication of *The Last of the Sailing Coasters*, I suggested to Edmund Eglinton that he should write such an account. Encouraged by the success of his earlier book he was ready to do so, but pointed out that such an account could not be history. Nobody knew, for example, exactly what was said by a particular ketch master of a particular vessel to the mate in conditions at a particular time. The book would have to be about an imaginary vessel and the description of her handling and of the men and their mutual relationships based closely on his own experience in over a decade of life in the vessels. He also pointed out that to put real hour-by-hour detail on record the description would have to be limited to a very brief period in the vessel's life—a week at the most—and contain accounts of contrasted problems: of those met with on an open sea passage and of the special difficulties of pilotage and ship handling in restricted tidal waters, both circumstances part of a vessel's normal working experience.

With his account of a week in the life of the imaginary *Mary Fletcher,* written when he was at the beginning of his eighties, Edmund Eglinton achieved exactly what he had set out to achieve—and died of a heart condition almost as soon as he had completed it.

Born on the levels protected from tidal flooding by the seabanks of the River Yeo in North Somerset at the beginning of this century, he began life working for his mason father on the maintenance of those same seabanks. Fascinated by the trows—local sailing barges of the inner Bristol Channel—which brought the stone for maintenance to the saltings below the seabanks from quarries adjacent to nearby tidalwater, he began his independent life by shipping as a hand in these vessels, from which he graduated to the ketch *Garlandstone* in the Irish trade (on which experience the passage home from Ireland in the *Mary Fletcher* is partly, but by no means entirely, based) and he went on to spend more than a decade in the 'vessels' of various kinds, some of it in command of the pretty little ketch *Lily*. Wishing eventually to marry, and faced with his potential wife's parents' challenge to settle down ashore, he re-entered the building trade (in the dark days following the Wall Street crash of 1929). He prospered, to spend his old age in a house of his own building on his own land exactly where he wanted it, with his 25–foot sailing yacht and his work shop in which he made the nameboards for my own boat and for the front yard gate of the farmhouse where this introduction is being written.

What sort of a man was the author of this account? My childhood touched on his life more than once and I knew him well. Without children, he and his wife were a devoted couple. Powerfully built and very skilful with his hands, he retained, when he wished to use it, the North Somerset dialect of his youth (and mine) to the end of his days. He used the old Germanic forms current in this part of the world until quite recently, 'Thee bist', 'Thee casn't', 'Thee snow', and the terminal 'l', so that the trow *Sarah,* in which he sailed, was invariably referred to as 'ole Sarol' (it is impossible to render the pronounciation of the 'o' vowel in this dialect, no other similar sound occurs except perhaps in Danish). Jamaica, which he had visited as a deck-hand in steamers was always Jamaicol, while my wife, Ann Giffard, became quite accustomed to being addressed as Annol. He was a very clever and determined man, but gentle and sensitive, a very jolly man who took life as he found it and enjoyed it to the full. He was outgoing and not self-regarding, despite the power of his total recall. He lived with zest.

Indeed, consciously or unconsciously, he has painted himself very well into the character of the mate of the *Mary Fletcher.* If you want to know what manner of man was the author of this book, ask George Cox.

Basil Greenhill

THE *MARY FLETCHER*

This study of the ketch *Heather Bell* gives a very good impression of the appearance of the *Mary Fletcher*. The *Heather Bell* was built at Barnstaple in 1870 and was photographed in October, 1920 , as she picked up a towline from the Lundy packet *Lerina* to bring her in over Appledore Bar in a calm. Ronald Tuck

Plate 1   *Snowflake*
This schooner was built at Runcorn on the Mersey in 1880 and is shown drying her mainsail, foresail, staysail standing jib and boom jib while discharging in Mevagissey, Cornwall, in the 1920s. When the *Mary Fletcher* was launched she was rigged like this vessel with two square sails on her foremast arranged as double topsails. H. Oliver Hill

CHAPTER 1

Early in the afternoon in the early days of November in the year 1925 old Georgie Morgan, a pensioner from the Cardiff Harbour Authorities, was walking along the foreshore of south Glamorganshire between Sully Island and the Lavernock point. He was exercising his dog, it was his favourite walk. Even in bad weather, if the wind was right, George would follow the high water mark with pleasant expectation, for there he was likely to find flotsam in plenty. Most of that day the wind had swept down from the eastward not far below gale force bringing thick driving rain, but now the wind had veered a couple of points southerly, an ideal wind to drive anything ashore that had been brought up on the flood tide past the isle of Sully

No chance of seeing Flatholm today, just over two miles to windward, but he could hear the two blasts from the fog siren, one long one short. Suddenly out of the mist, to the south'ard loomed a ship, not much more than half a mile off the shore and, as her outline became clearer, old George could see she was a ketch on the starboard tack. She was well reefed down too, the jaws of her main and mizzen gaffs appeared to be halfway down their respective masts.

Out there in the mist she appeared to be hump-backed, but as she shortened the distance between herself and the shore, the watcher realised the vessel was carrying deck cargo. She was 'light on' in the water, and the flood tide sweeping her up against the strong wind, together with the deck cargo, gave her a tendency to heel over—considering she was reefed down—more than she should.

Now seemingly to swell in size as she rapidly approached the shore, George could make out the white ends of sawn logs, telling him she was loaded with pitprops.

The master evidently knew what he was about, standing on until the ship was within a cable's length of Sully Island, the helm was put down, the masts became upright, the headsails thrashing, then the main and the mizzen: George could see two men forward, one making fast the jib sheet—for only the standing jib was set—and one standing by the staysail bowline, ready to let it draw as

3

Plate 2   *Maud Mary* and *Hobah*
The ketches *Maud Mary*, built at Howden Dyke in 1889, and *Hobah*, built at Trelew Creek, Mylor, Cornwall in 1879, lying moored off the Richmond Drydock at Appledore. They are both just resting on the ground as the tide ebbs. H. Oliver Hill

soon as the vessel head passed the eye of the wind.

Now she was round and, lying over on the port tack was soon lost to sight in the wintry mist.

George did not envy those fellows that wet cold and windy November day. As a lad in his 'teens he had served in those small vessels. But that was nearly fifty years ago when these ships could afford full crews; even then the work was notoriously hard, the lack of sleep, and the resulting weariness of body and mind still an unpleasant memory.

The vessel which had claimed old George's attention was the ketch *Mary Fletcher* of Bideford. Built in the 1870s in Cornwall and then rigged as a double topsail two masted schooner (Plate 1), she had a carrying capacity of 130 tons. Her draught aft was 11′ 0″, her draught forward two feet less. Bought by Appledore owners in the 1890s she had immediately been re-rigged as an efficient ketch (Plates 2, 3, 4, & 5) which saved one man in the crew and was cheaper to maintain though slower down wind than she had been as a schooner. That late afternoon as she disappeared into the gloom of the channel, Captain Henry Trumper of Appledore, the vessel's master, and part owner, called to the mate to look out for the buoy. 'Aye, Aye,' called the mate, who was already keeping a sharp look out, for he knew the buoy referred to—the Wolves light buoy about two miles off the weather bow marking the Wolves rocks. 'We'll give her another five minutes, George, then put her about, buoy or no buoy!'

Plate 3 *Garlandstone*
The account of the *Mary Fletcher*'s passage from Kinsale to Cardiff is based partly on the author's experiences as mate of the ketch *Garlandstone* built at Bere Ferrers, Devon, in 1909. This photograph showing many details on deck in the *Garlandstone* was taken in 1937. Basil Greenhill

Plate 4   *Garlandstone*
The underwater body of the *Garlandstone* as she lies dried out on the ebb tide in an Irish harbour.
Note the propeller— she has an auxiliary engine and an extension added to the rudder to make her
easier to steer under power. Michael Leszczynski

Plate 5   *H. F. Bolt*
The ketch *H. F. Bolt*, built at Bideford in 1876 and named for the two daughters, Harriet and
Florence, of her master and part owner, Captain Bolt, was the last westcountry coasting ketch to
earn her living at sea without an engine. In appearance she closely resembles the *Mary Fletcher*. She
has a jib headed topsail set flying from the deck, Appledore worm roller reefing gear on both masts,
and a whaleback wheel shelter, but she has no galley or whaleback lavatory shelter on deck—for
which see Plates 33 and 34. Her sails from foreward aft were named the flying jib, boom jib, standing
jib staysail, mainsail, topsail, mizzen, and mizzen topsail—which latter sail the *Mary Fletcher* did
not have. The *H. F. Bolt* was accidentally destroyed when laid up at Appledore during the Second
World War. Vernon Boyle

The mate's name was George Cox. A native of Somerset, he had been brought up in the Severn trows, the local sailing barges (Plate 6), before serving in vessels that traded outside the Bristol Channel, and was well acquainted with the hazards of that part of the channel above the Holms. The master went the few steps back to the galley to warn the able seaman, who was preparing the supper, to stand by the staysail bowline ready to go about. His name was Arthur Ferryman. He belonged to Ilfracombe and eight of his twenty-two years had been spent in the vessels, that is, the ketches and schooners, mostly the 'down homers' as they were locally known, ketches that traded over Bideford Bar eastwards to the ports and harbour of the Bristol Channel and rarely sailed westwards into the open Atlantic.

Plate 6 *Gloster Packet, Oliver* and *Providence*
The open moulded trow *Gloster Packet* on the grids in the Bridgwater River. She was built at Stroud in 1824, and is under repair. Her caulking is being hardened in and her masts have been unstepped and sent ashore, probably for replacement. Astern of her are the flush decked trow *Oliver*, built at Hempstead, Gloucestershire, in 1871, and the open moulded trow *Providence*, built at Gloucester in 1824. The latter is discharging cargo into carts by means of a hand winch. Note that the *Providence* has a topsail stowed aloft, and that she and the *Oliver* both have staysail booms, like the *Mary Fletcher*. From an old postcard

Plate 7   Galley
The cook about to enter the galley of the schooner *Result*. These galleys were not fixed to the decks
of the vessels but secured to ringbolts with iron rods and straps tightened with nuts on threads.
These can be seen clearly. Basil Greenhill

'About time too!', said Arthur, 'Us am nearly choked with smoke with her on
this here tack.' This was a common trouble with the coasting vessels, for the
galley was usually abaft the mainmast (Plate 7) with tho flue at the mercy of the
down draft from the mainsail. Wherever the chimney of the galley range was
situated it usually gave trouble on one tack or the other, and this varied
according to the strength of the wind. The cowl on the top of the flue pipe would
sometimes help, but in a strong wind the down draught invariably won, and that
day the wind indeed was strong.

'Ready about! Ease up the jib sheet,' came the call from aft. Captain Trumper
spun the wheel to windward putting the helm down as George eased a couple of
feet of sheet to spill the wind from the jib.

The *Mary Fletcher,* as a result of her speed, seemed to fly up into the wind, her
bow leaping up as it encountered an extra high oncoming sea which, although
nothing to worry about, flung a heavy shower of white spray over the foredeck,
blinding the mate for a second or two, the sudden icy cold causing him to gasp
and splutter, whilst he strove to control the now wildly flailing jib sheet, the
heavy *lignum vitae* bullseye, attached as it was to the chain part of the sheet,
whizzing through the air, and from which one blow would break a man's skull.

The ship was nearly in the eye of the wind now and still turning fast. Arthur, the A.B., seeing the mate's discomfiture owing to the dousing he had received, had run to the opposite jib sheet and whipped a turn around the port bitt fearing it might get out of control (Plate 8). But the mate was only two or three seconds behind him, both of them quickly tautening down the jib now rapidly filling. 'Thanks, Art' said the mate, 'See to the bowline!'

The staysail was now just aback. Arthur seeing the jib fill took the turns of the bowline off its belaying pin, on the starboard rail the boom of the sail flew across the deck with an almighty bang, the big shackle of the heavy chain sheet attached to the boom end rasping and striking fire on the iron fore horse.

Many of the vessels did not have a staysail boom but Captain Trumper would not be without one. He contended that with a boom a staysail would back more quickly, the foot of the sail being stretched taut along the boom, thus pushing a ship around more speedily when tacking.

From the moment the Captain called to his crew 'ready about', until Arthur the A.B. cast off the staysail bowline from its pin, no more than two minutes of time would have passed, for a ketch with plenty of wind does not 'hesitate' in stays—unlike a topsail schooner which is inclined to 'hang' in stays immediately her topsails are aback.

Plate 8 *Emma Louise*
This photograph of the foredeck of the ketch *Emma Louise*, built at Barnstaple in 1881, shows the forehatch with a heavy hawser coiled on it, the forecastle scuttle, the forecastle stove chimney pipe with its cowl, the windlass and the chain cable and the inboard end of the bowsprit with the staysail resting on it, but not made fast. The two mooring ropes, leading outboard over the warping chocks, are secured around the windlass bitts and the windlass ends in the way the standing jib sheets of the *Mary Fletcher* are described in the text as having been temporarily secured to prevent the jib passing out of control when putting the ketch through the wind. Basil Greenhill

Plate 9   Wheelhouse
The wheelhouse, or, more correctly, the whaleback wheel shelter. The vessel is the ketch *Hobah* (see Plate 2) of Bideford with her master, Captain William Lamey, posing at the open wheel. Basil Greenhill

Suddenly fine over the starboard quarter George Cox thought he saw a flash, but the driving mist was heavier now. There it was again. Walking back to the waist he told the Captain. 'Take over for a few minutes then George', said the skipper. As George took the helm they both saw another flash, they were nearer than they expected to be, such is the deception of thick weather at sea where no objects are available to calculate distance.

The tide, sweeping them up, soon they were abreast of the buoy, the Wolves buoy.

Captain Trumper said, 'Keep her off a bit George, keep her due north till I come back, I'm going up to the bucket!' The 'bucket' as Captain Trumper termed it was the ship's lavatory. It was situated just forward of the fore rigging on the port side, not in the wheelhouse aft as in most vessels of that class. Incidentally, the wheelhouses did not accommodate the wheel, they were store places for navigation lights and (if not a toilet) a lock up place for paints, brushes and buckets. Actually the helmsmen stood in front of the wheelhouse which was really a shelter against the vessel being overtaken by a following sea breaking on board (Plate 9). The wheel itself was on the open after deck. The wheelhouse sheltered the helmsman somewhat from a following wind.

The Captain had needed the 'bucket', as he called it, while the ship was on the other tack, the port tack, but that would have meant using that accommodation when it was to windward, and, as whoever used the bucket had to empty it himself, the captain would have had to cross the slanting deck to empty the receptacle to leeward. Not a very dignified journey on that wet and windy day, with the decks cluttered up with pitprops.

The lavatory was a timber structure just over two feet square and, having a whale back, was not too unattractive. The door could be bolted on the inside. The seat was varnished oak with a hole in it, and the galvanised bucket stood within a timber ring on the deck. The sides, back and front of that 'office' did not reach the deck, but stood on four iron legs about four inches high bolted to the deck; this allowed the 'floor' to be washed down whenever the deck was. The Captain, his bucket emptied and replaced half full of water within its ring, went aft to the wheel. They were now nearing the West Cardiff grounds buoy opposite Lavernock Point.

'All right George', said the Captain, 'We'll go in on the mud I think, keep near the mouth of Ely river, what do you think?' 'Yes', said George 'we'll be snug enough there on the mud', but the mate knew the Captain was only being polite. Had he opposed that plan of action it would have made no difference.

'Better get the anchor off the rail then I reckon', said George, 'Bit smoother in here thank God.' 'Aye, get everything ready George.' Passing the galley on his way forward the mate looked in the lee door. He saw the huge oval stock pot, its lid lifting and trembling, the steam weaving about, giving off such a wonderful appetising aroma that can only be appreciated to the full by wet cold and hungry men. In that pot he well knew was boiled beef, all kinds of root vegetables, dough boys—even a plum duff, as it was called which contained no plums but raisins and currants mixed with plain flour and suet.

'All ready I see Arthur', said the mate, nodding towards the stockpot, 'come and give us a hand to get the anchor ready, and the bobstay slacked off. Only about a mile and a half to go now.' 'Not much rest aboard this bugger!', said Arthur. 'Just cleaned the cabin up and filled the coal bucket and soon's the anchor's down you and the old man will be hollering for supper! He'll have to get a cook, a fourth hand!' Going forward together George said, 'Bin a rough trip this time Art. She's certainly heavy. Plenty of room for another hand, if only a boy for the galley.' Actually both men were wacked out. It had been a most aggravating and laborious trip.

CHAPTER 2

No other cargo being available, the *Mary Fletcher* at the beginning of the passage of which the final hours have been described had loaded pitprops in Kinsale Harbour for Cardiff (Plate 10). These were stowed both in the hold and on deck, whence they were very carefully secured with rope lashings, though there were a few loose logs on top.

Leaving the ancient Irish harbour in the early morning with the wind north by east Captain Trumper set the course due east. On that course they would, if the wind held, pick up St Goven's Head on the Pembrokeshire coast giving them a weather shore even if the wind veered somewhat, or backed to the north west. The only snag, of course, was that there were a hundred and twenty miles of water between the *Mary Fletcher* and the coast of Wales. At the moment the wind was about a point forward of the beam and, although it was only a fresh wind, the deck cargo tended to cause the ship to roll more than she should. What if the wind increased? As soon as the vessel was clear of the harbour the mate had streamed the log and chalked the time and course down on a piece of flat asbestos—in 1925 there was no knowledge of how dangerous this material really is. Twenty years earlier they would have used a slate. Should a change of wind come, necessitating an alteration of course, the log would be hauled in and reset and the mileage recorded on the asbestos together with the time and the new course. All very elementary, but quite effective for short coastal work.

The log itself was a torpedo shaped tube about eighteen inches long with fins on a sleeve affair at the rear which revolved in accordance with the speed of the ship through the water. The revolutions caused dials to rotate within the log registering the sea miles travelled. The log however had to be hauled aboard to be read—sometimes alas, to find seaweed had fouled the fins.

No one had ever seen a patent log (as they were called) fixed to the taffrail of a coasting sailer. They were expensive things which looked like clocks and were fixed to a fitting on the rail. There the log line itself, driven by the fixed fins on the log being towed, revolved indicating the speed and mileage for all to see. New fangled of course!

Plate 10   Loading Pitprops
The three-masted schooner *Cambourne*, built at Amlwch in 1885, loading pitprops in an Irish river.
Bernard Shaw

After coiling away all the halyards and hanging them clear of the deck ready for running when occasion arose (Plate 11), the mate and the able seaman had dragged the main gaff topsail up from the fore peak, bent on the halyard, rove the jackstay through the hanks on the luff outweather of the sail and bent on the tack and the sheet, thus getting the sail ready to be set (Plate 12). George Cox, the mate, carried out that exercise with the help of the able seaman without any orders from the master. George was a competent mate. His job was to get things done without bothering the Captain. What he would not do in doubtful circumstances would be to hoist the topsail without permission. So now, looking at the sky to windward first, he turned with a look of inquiry to Captain Trumper at the wheel; a negative wave of the hand was all the reply he needed. Putting a gasket around the gear attached to the topsail, he secured it against the wind to the foot of the mast.

Ten years before, that topsail would have been stowed aloft, but the 1914 war had taken most of the young men out of the 'vessels' into the navy, and stowing a gaff topsail aloft called for men with much agility and intrepidity (Plate 13); it was a one man job riding a gaff topsail down, wrapping a gasket around it, the heavy canvas billowing and banging in a strong wind causing such trembling of the mast that it could be felt throughout the ship. The *Mary Fletcher*'s topsail contained over 400 square feet of canvas. The post-war period brought less trade,

less skilled hands, and the auxiliary motor ship, so that few topsails were ever
again stowed aloft, simply because sufficient hands could not be afforded, even
if they had been available, to work the ships, and, with the auxiliary motors,
topsails were used less and less. In a few years' time many pole masted motor
ketches would not even have them.

Everything tidy aboard now. Arthur Ferryman went into the galley to rake
the fire and attend to his other duties as cook. The mate walked forward and,
tearing a loose piece of bark from one of the pit props, cast it over the side to
windward just abaft the billboard. The fact that he had to trot along the deck to
keep up with it as the vessel swept past the nearly submerged bark indicated
their speed through the water was about six knots. 'Doing about six I'd say',
puffed the mate as he stopped by the Captain, for he'd had to hop over some of
the deck cargo during his twenty odd yards back to the wheel. 'Six and a half I
reckon', replied the Captain, 'Had the deck been clear you'd have kept up with it
George!' They were aware that this rough and ancient method of testing the
speed of a vessel, though a guide, could never be accurate. At twelve noon the log

Plate 11   Starboard Rigging of the Mainmast
'After coiling away all the halyards and hanging them clear of the deck ready for running when
occasion arose . . ..' On board the ketch *Clara May*, built at Plymouth in 1891, four shrouds set up
with dead eyes and lanyards can be seen. The main halyards are belayed round a pin through the
cavils and the remainder hung up on the sheerpole. Basil Greenhill

would be hauled in, the knots recorded and a faint line pencilled on the chart in the cabin.

Meanwhile the wind was freshening, lying the vessel over and putting her gunwale in the water. 'Good job we never set your topsail George', said the Captain. The mate did not reply to that statement, saying instead, 'Expect you've got some writing to do below Cap'n? Is the course still east?' 'Yes', replied the Captain, standing aside to let George take the wheel, 'I have a feeling this wind will veer more easterly. Wouldn't like it to head us off before we make the coast with this clutter around the deck.' The mate had to agree, although he knew a more southerly course would have taken them more quickly up the Bristol Channel.

In the galley Arthur was trimming the side lights and stern light. They would be put back in the wheel house ready to be lit and put up at sunset. Before he stowed them away however it was cocoa time, 10 a.m. Quickly ladling a level tablespoonful of cocoa into each of two pint mugs and filling them with boiling water from the ever-ready kettle on the range, Arthur took them back to the cabin.

'Well done Arthur', said the Captain, 'didn't realise it was ten o'clock yet!', this in spite of the fact that the cabin clock and barometer were within four feet of him. Captain Trumper was standing up in the entrance to his little room off the main cabin (Plate 14) stropping his open razor. Facing forward, as he was, with the strong breeze blowing on the port side of the vessel, meant his right leg was stretched rigidly down to leeward (for the Master's room is always to starboard) his left leg acting as flexible buttress, keeping his body perpendicular and counteracting the lurches of the ship to leeward owing to the lively beam sea. But the mirror on the bulkhead, swinging across his vision with every roll, could not be stilled, it was a shaving snag that only practice could overcome. Going on deck Arthur moved to the weather side of the mate to take over the helm while George went below to drink his cocoa; for the mate's quarters were also in a room off the cabin, a little smaller, but not much smaller, than the Captain's—it was, of course, on the port side.

'East it is, Art', said the mate, 'She's popping along mind, wants quite a bit of weather helm!' 'Garge', said Arthur looking up at the sky to windward 'I never sid a vessel spend more time on the port tack than this bugger!!' That ridiculous statement, and the look of disgust on Arthur's face, so tickled the mate that he was unable to control his mirth and, when stepping down off the grating, he fumbled his feet just as the ship rolled to leeward and slid down into the scuppers.

Left Plate 12   *Buttercup*
In this photograph the ketch *Buttercup*, built at Goole in 1884 but owned in Falmouth and rigged in westcountry style, has a jib headed topsail which sets flying from the deck exactly as described in the *Mary Fletcher*. The iron hanks can be seen in position on the weather of the sail with the wire jackstay running down them to the deck from about six or seven feet above the iron cap of the main mast. H. Oliver Hill

Plate 14   *Kathleen & May*
The cabin of the schooner *Kathleen & May*, of Bideford, now preserved in London River, when she was a working vessel. The cabin of the *Mary Fletcher* was almost identical in layout and fittings. Looking forward the entrance to the master's room is to starboard. It was here that Captain Trumper stood shaving (chapter 2) looking in a mirror that would have been by the side of the oil lamp visible here. The knob of the door of the mate's room is just visible on the extreme left. The door on the port side of the fireplace leads to the foot of the companion. The starboard bench on which master and mate dossed down in their clothes in bad weather can be seen by the table at which all the crew ate. The cabin stove has been replaced with a paraffin convection heater. Basil Greenhill

This, and the fluent abuse the mate gave voice to, even though it included calling him the 'silliest bastard in Combe (Ilfracombe)' filled Arthur with boisterous delight. His guffaws brought the Captain's head up above the scuttle coaming with, 'What's the joke then, you two?' 'Joke', replied the mate, 'I nearly went over the side owing to that fool! and what does he do? Whickers like some bloody gurt hoss!' 'Your cocoas will be cold', exclaimed Arthur, for he wanted a cup himself and after the warmth of the galley it was cold at the wheel. He had made his remark about the ship always being on the port tack because it was his contention that the galley chimney always refused to draw properly when the wind was on the port side—the port tack.

Having drunk his cocoa with the Captain, the mate returned to the deck to take the helm. As they changed places he handed Arthur the two cocoa mugs,

Left Plate 13   Topsail Stowed Aloft
The vessel, of which the main gaff topsail has been so tightly and properly stowed aloft, is the barquentine *Waterwitch*, of Fowey, the last square rigged merchant sailing ship ever to work out of a home port in Britain. Philip L. Welford

Plate 15   Discharging by Hand Winch (1)
The two man crew of the Scots trading smack *Anna Bahn*, at the hand winch discharging aggregate from Oban at Tobermory in 1946. A third man, hired from the shore, works the wheelbarrow. Basil Greenhill

'Thought it would save you a journey, Art. Still on the port tack I see!', he added, his eyes full of mischief.

The *Mary Fletcher* was about eighty feet long over taffrail and stemhead. Her bowsprit end stood out nearly twenty five feet clear of the stem and carried three jibs, the standing jib, the boom jib and the flying jib. Unlike a good few of the ships of her class, she had no motor winch, but just the dolly winch, worked by two cranked handles and the power of two men. In isolated rivers and harbours where there were no unloading facilities ashore, the crew and the dolly winch comprised the only available method of discharging and it was not at all unusual for cargo after cargo to be unloaded in this way (Plate 15).

A ship could arrive at a harbour in the early hours of the morning after a hard and stormy passage, the crew unshaven, weary and red-eyed from lack of sleep, yet the hatches had to be off, the unloading gear aloft, and the gang plank in position ready for the merchants' people, hauliers, etc., to start work at 8 a.m. (Plate 16). The crew then had to winch out the cargo and get it over the side by their own manpower.

When the *Mary Fletcher* was built and rigged as a schooner, fifty years before

Plate 16   Discharging by Hand Winch (2)
The ketch *New Design*, built at Bridgwater in 1871, discharging coal from South Wales at St Ives into carts. Note the topsail stowed aloft, the open wheel without wheel shelter, the whalebacked lavatory box in the way of the mizzen shrouds on the port side and the galley on deck. This photograph is perhaps more than one hundred years old. Royal Institution of Cornwall

this passage in 1925, she would have had at least five hands aboard; if the Master was elderly, probably six hands. But in 1925 an elderly Captain and two hands had to do everything: load her, sail her home from Ireland, and, often discharge her.

But nevertheless that day on her easterly course to St Goven's Head, the *Mary Fletcher* was a happy ship. The crew had been lucky to have an 'all night in' the

night before in Kinsale Harbour. It had been well after dark when the last pit
props were put aboard, the lamps on the quay giving just enough light to show
the loader and crew to stow the last of the cargo. Now it was nearing dinner time
and at noon Arthur would bring the dinner back to the cabin. He would then
take the wheel again while the Captain and the mate enjoyed his cooking.
Today the menu was the hotted up remains of the roast beef from the day before,
and the usual dish of vegetables.

    The Captain usually carved the joint and dished out whatever else there was.
Unlike some masters in those vessels, Captain Trumper believed in plenty of
'victuals'. He was careful too, never to put more on his own plate than on any
other. There was a side oven in the cabin fireplace and here the midday dinner
for the man at the wheel was kept hot. At a few minutes before noon, Captain
Trumper went on deck to haul in the log. Quickly hauling it in, before he gave
the necessary twist of the wrist to expose the dials, looking at the mate at the
helm he said, 'How many George!', 'Twenty-five!', said George, 'Just what I was
going to say', said the Captain. Giving the cylinder a twist he exclaimed, 'Both
wrong George! Its 27, all but about a cable'. The *Mary Fletcher* had not done
badly, making an average of nearly six and three quarter knots. But it was still
nearly a hundred miles to St Goven's Head. Below in his room the Captain
entered the distance, together with the time, on his own small slate with a frame
hung on the bulkhead. The course not being altered, there was no need to bother
with the chart for the moment. Then Arthur's feet appeared. He was coming
down the companion ladder with his elbows jutting out to steady himself against
the brass handrails of the ladder, for he had the deep sided meat dish in his
hands containing the hotted up joint. Although the table was listing with the
ship, the fiddle around the edges prevented any slide off to leeward. Dumping the
meat dish to the side of the table, Arthur went forward again for the vegetable
dish. Meantime the Captain had taken the hot plates from the cabin oven and he
was carving the joint when the cook returned. 'Well done Arthur', said the
Captain, 'I'll put yours in the oven first of all. George won't be sorry to be
relieved. We'll not be long boy!' In that way Captain Trumper let Arthur know
he was pleased with his promptitude, that keeping his dinner hot was of first
importance, and that George at the wheel would be glad of a warm. This
considerate attitude towards his crew of two arose not only because he was a
kind man by nature, but also because he knew he had two good men and he
wanted them to be contented, so that they would stay with the *Mary Fletcher*,
even though the trade at the time would not allow him to pay better wages, or to
carry that extra hand that would have made all the difference in their hours of
sleep.

    The mate came stumping down the companion ladder, stiff with the cold and
blowing into his hands: 'She's popping along a bit Cap'n,' he said, 'If the wind
holds we could be in the lee of the land by daylight tomorrow'. Nodding his head
the Captain replied, 'If this wind freshens George it may be good policy to put a

couple of rolls in the mainsail before dark, better than fumbling about, with the decks as they are, in the darkness.' 'Aye, Aye', said the mate, 'save having to call Arthur out.'

If at all possible on a passage the 'cook' as he was called, was allowed to have a full night's rest. Thus during the day he was able to attend to all the galley chores; keep the cabin clean and tidy, pump the ship out if necessary (most wooden vessels, especially when sailing in a strong wind, would make a certain amount of water). Then there were the navigation lights to be trimmed and refilled, and the master and mate to be relieved at the wheel for their meal times. There was plenty of work to keep a man busy most of the daylight hours.

In the cabin the Captain and mate had finished their dinner. The mate poured water into the teapot left ready by the cook; there was always a kettle of hot water ready on the cabin range. A dinner whether hot or cold would be unthinkable unless followed by the inevitable pint mug of tea. But a Bideford vessel did not feed the crew once inside Appledore Bar. Had the *Mary Fletcher* gone into her home port the kettle would have come off the stove as she sailed into the river.

During that typical repast in the cabin of the *Mary Fletcher* both men's eyes flashed a glance from time to time upwards to the skylight that let daylight into the cabin, for the ship had a 'tell tale' compass. This compass had two cards. The top one of course was for the helmsman. The other could be seen through the skylight from the cabin, the binnacle being fixed conveniently to serve both purposes.

This arrangement kept whoever was at the helm 'on his toes'. Even the Captain, if he knew the mate was in the cabin, tended to be more careful, lest he set a bad example.

The Captain, draining his teacup, went into his room and struggled into his winter overcoat, for he would now take over the wheel from Arthur the cook for an hour or two, for, having had all night in last night, the watches would be set later.

'She's swinging about a bit Cap'n', said Arthur as the Captain took over the helm. The wind was less steady now, and a sudden gust would sometimes drive the ship's head up to windward before it could be effectively checked by the helm. 'We could feel that down below, Arthur', replied the Captain, 'But I noticed you caught her quick enough and brought her back over, making things even; better than I shall do I reckon'.

'Hello Art', said the mate as Arthur stepped off the ladder into the cabin, 'We thought you were putting her about once or twice!!' But Arthur was used to the good natured quips from his shipmate, for he knew, to use his own expression, 'they contained nary a bit of malice'.

Arthur was clearing away the dinner things when from the deck they both heard the Captain call out 'Sail-ho!'. Going on deck they saw away off the port bow about two or three miles, a double topsail schooner, her outline blurred by the afternoon haze. Soon they could see she was a three-master, and that her fore and aft foresail was tanned. 'Get the binoculars Arthur,' said the Captain, 'I think I know her, its the old *Enterprize,* out of Youghal or Dungarvan I expect, bound around the Land'. (That is Land's End. The schooner was bound for a port up the English Channel.)

When Arthur appeared with the binoculars the Captain nodding towards the schooner said 'You have a look at her Arthur—tell us what you think of her'. The cook, trying to keep his body upright whilst the ship lurched and heaved beneath him, said, 'She's light on Cap'n. Oats I suppose. God, but she's travelling, all foaming white round her bows!'

'That's the *Enterprize* alright,' said Captain Trumper. 'Her skipper and I were shipmates twenty years ago. His name's Bob Slocombe. He doesn't own her—too fond of the tiddly. But he's a good master; drives her around!' Meanwhile the two ships were now, although their courses were at right angles, rapidly approaching each other. Now they could see the hoops of her fore and aft sails, standing clearly out against the shining pitchpine of the three masts; visible too were the hanks of the jibs on their respective stays.

The *Enterprize*—for she it was—with her booms out to port, the wind slightly on her starboard quarter, and her Plimsoll line well out of the water, seemed to be coming down upon them with the speed of a train, yet her speed could not have been above eight and a half knots. The *Mary Fletcher,* close hauled on the port tack, was on the 'wrong tack' as it was termed. The tack on which a sailing vessel, to conform with the rules, gave way to a vessel on the starboard tack. But the *Enterprize* had a fair wind, and vessels with a fair wind should always give way to ships close hauled.

To the crew of the *Mary Fletcher,* however, it appeared as if the latter rule was being ignored. George Cox sprang up from where he was sitting on the cabin skylight, cast an anxious look at the Captain and exclaimed 'Surely they must have seen us?' Arthur the cook, feeling the schooner must certainly ram them right amidships, grasped the after shroud of the mizzen rigging, sprang upon the top gallant rail and, waving his free arm in the air, shouted 'Keep her away you bloody fools!' 'Shut up Arthur! Come down boy!' said the Captain, but he too was apprehensive, thinking that if he put his helm up and turned his vessel's stern, a smaller target, towards the on coming ship they might get crushed if the *Enterprize*'s bow smashed into their counter.

They could read the name *Enterprize* easily now, not much more than a cable's length away. Two faces could be seen looking over the starboard bow, and two muffled figures on the after deck, one at the helm. From the deck of the *Mary*

Right Plate 17   *Jane Banks*
'From the deck of the *Mary Fletcher* the long and shiny bowsprit of the schooner, pointing at a sharp angle skywards one moment, and the next dipping down menacingly, was a chilling sight to the crew of the little ketch, momentarily expecting to be overwhelmed.' The three-masted schooner *Jane Banks*, ex *Frau Minna Petersen*, built at Porthmadog in 1878, a vessel of the same size and rig as the fictional *Enterprize*. Graham Gullick

Fletcher the long and shiny bowsprit of the schooner, pointing at a sharp angle skywards at one moment, the next dipping down menacingly, was a chilling sight to the crew of the little ketch, momentarily expecting to be overwhelmed (Plate 17). All this happened in a very few moments of time, a dramatic change from a picture of beauty to a vision of destruction and calamity.

Captain Trumper, his eyes rivetted upon the two figures on the quarter deck, suddenly saw the man at the wheel bend low as he spun the wheel to starboard and furiously kept pulling at the spokes to put the helm hard down. The schooner responded simultaneously, her head rearing and dipping as she swung to starboard, her bowsprit end clearing the mizzen rigging of the *Mary Fletcher* by less than twenty feet. But the ketch was travelling ahead, her stern now clear of the stabbing bowsprit. For a moment Captain Trumper thought the stern of the *Enterprize,* swinging down by the momentum of the turn, would strike the smaller ship's quarter, but a reversal of the helm stopped the swing and the *Enterprize* swept past the stern of the smaller vessel, her boom ends only a few feet clear of the counter of her near victim. Added to the unbelievable and fear-inspiring sight of a ship seemingly racing down towards them, bent on the destruction of their ship, maybe even of both ships, down wind as the crew of the *Mary Fletcher* was, the roar of the water displaced by the schooner's bows and the whistling and droning of the wind through her lofty sails and spars was a sound that each one of them would never forget, even though the period of time was only seconds, for a ship travelling at 8 knots covers 266 yards in one minute.

Captain Trumper, still hanging on to the wheel, turned to look at the two men on the quarter deck of the *Enterprize,* his face white with fury. He got a fleeting glimpse of two red and hilarious faces, one the bovine face of his old shipmate Bob Slocombe. The latter waved his hat, and was shouting something, but the only words the crew of the *Mary Fletcher* heard was 'Come on Hurry', evidently directed at Captain Trumper. Looking at his two crew members the Captain said, 'Those fellows were drunk as Lords!'

The mate, looking at the fast receding ship with angry eyes, said, 'I'd prefer to call them mad dogs and I'd like to see them treated as such.' 'I expect they were ashore in Youghal this morning, if they've come from there. Or maybe they had a drunken night and brought some bottles aboard for a livener today', said the Captain.

Arthur, his colour now returned and looking at the Captain said, 'Shall I make some more tea? the kettle's still boiling.' 'The quicker, the better Arthur! It'll take the nasty taste of those drunken sods out of our mouths', then to the mate Captain Trumper said 'Haul in the log George, it's now one o'clock, it should be showing about 34 miles, but we'd better be sure for I intend to mark this reading off on the chart.' 'You're going to report him then Cap'n,' said George. 'I have a mind to George', said the master. 'I feel I ought to. What's your opinion?' 'Waste of time I reckon', said the Mate 'they would swear blind it was untrue, its their word ag'in ours, best to forget it.'

Then, hauling in the log hand over hand George swung it up over the taffrail and, with the dexterity of much practice, twisted it open to expose the dials. 'A couple of cables short of 34 Cap'n', said George and, stepping over beside the Captain at the wheel he took over the helm to allow Captain Trumper to go to his room and mark off the chart. Thus ended an experience the three men were to recall with wonder for the rest of their lives, an experience none of them wished to undergo again.

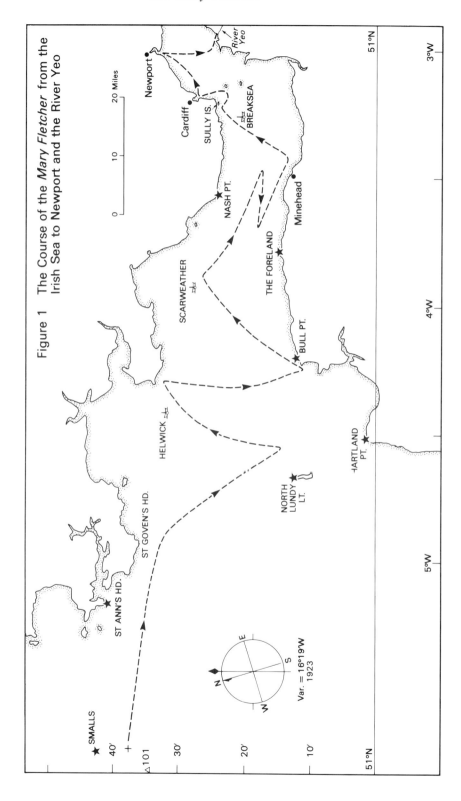

Figure 1   The Course of the *Mary Fletcher* from the Irish Sea to Newport and the River Yeo

CHAPTER 3

At eleven o'clock that same night the mate lifted the Smalls light, he had seen the loom of it nearly an hour before. He estimated by the time they were abeam of the triple flash light it would be about six miles to windward. Time enough to ease the sheets off and point her head a bit more southerly when Captain Trumper took over the wheel at midnight.

Coming on deck just before twelve o'clock, that is when the *Mary Fletcher* was 16 hours out from Kinsale, Captain Trumper said 'Couldn't seem to get off to sleep George, couldn't stop thinking of the *Enterprize*. No one will believe it.' 'It'll get around though', replied the mate, 'if we keep silent, you can bet Slocombe's crew in the fo'c'sle will spread it around, they must have thought they'd had it too!' Taking over the helm the Captain said 'Haul the log in George, should be reading about a hundred, not bad for sixteen hours on one tack.' The reading was a hundred and one it had to be by the position of the Smalls.

The loom of St Anns Head could now be seen. They did not bother to stream the log again. The main and mizzen sheets were eased off and, steering S.E. by E. the *Mary Fletcher,* with the wind now abaft the beam, behaved more comfortably, the monotonous roll cut by half. The mate now went below, took off his heavy outer deck clothes and likewise his boots, laid his great coat on the cabin locker to lie on his small coat to form a pillow. Before lying down however he drank a big mug of tea— made by the Captain and left standing in the teapot on the hob of the cabin fireplace.

In such circumstances, especially at night, the mate—or the Captain—would not use their bunks in their respective rooms, their main reason being that the man at the wheel might at any time want some help on deck in a hurry. If he was in his room the man below could not hear so easily. By using the cabin locker he could lie down in his trousers and jersey, even if they were wet, ready at any time to spring up and reach the deck in a few seconds, should there be a sudden change of wind. Or, if the ship was on the port tack and a red light appeared on

29

Plate 18   *Bessie Ellen*
The ketch *Bessie Ellen*, built at Plymouth in 1907, off St Anns Head in 1940. She is sailing north west to avoid a wartime minefield, the exact whereabouts of which was uncertain. She has been fitted with an auxiliary motor, and her masts have been poled off—she has no topmast—and her bowsprit shortened. Both her topsail and her flying jib have been done away with. Basil Greenhill

Plate 19   *Kathleen & May*
'Soon there was no weight on the helm, the booms swung amidships with the roll of the ship.' *Kathleen & May* becalmed in a heavy swell off St Goven's Head, 1959. Basil Greenhill

the starboard bow, which meant that a vessel on the starboard tack was approaching on a converging course, the ship might have to be put about and quickly.

By the time George had drunk his tea and smoked a cigarette it was half an hour after midnight. In three and a half hours he would be at the helm again. True they had all had a full night in the night before, but by eight o'clock the next day he, the mate, would have managed only less than four hours' sleep. Yet men like him, his shipmate, Arthur, and the Captain himself, even though they knew their lot was unlikely to improve, still clung to the little ships they had grown to cherish and to the exercise of the highly developed skills they had acquired on board them. No power on earth, however, would have persuaded any one of them to admit to that fact.

Captain Trumper shouted down the companion way to wake the mate at ten minutes to four a.m. This gave George time to make a pot of tea, enough for both of them, and to drink his before going on deck. Drinking his tea he noticed there was nothing like so much motion and he put this down to the ship being now in the shelter of the land.

On deck he found the wind had eased and that the ship had her booms aboard again. Whilst George was below the vessel had only covered about eighteen miles, for they were now just abreast of St Anns Head (Plate 18). 'Why didn't you call me, Cap'n?', said George, 'Oh, I managed alright', was the answer, 'don't forget I had the first watch below. The wind had eased, the becket on the wheel was enough'. 'There's plenty of tea in the pot', said George. By 5.30 that morning the *Mary Fletcher* was about three miles off St Goven's Head and under that bold rugged shore the wind, which had been so constant for the last twenty-four hours, seemed to waver. Soon there was no weight on the helm, the booms swung amidships with the roll of the ship (Plate 19). The racket caused by the slatting sails and the rattling of the heavy sheet blocks (Plate 20) brought the Captain's head up the companion way.

'Wind seems to want to head us off Cap'n', said the mate. Both men then felt a draught from the eastward. The jibs flapped and filled, the booms swung out, George felt the pressure on the helm as the ship gathered a little way, they were still on the port tack, but looking away from the land. 'How's her head George?', asked the Captain, and when told it was S.S.E. added 'Let her go off then, plenty of room out there.'

Down again Captain Trumper took a quick look at the chart. Lundy Island was twenty-five miles away on the course they were heading. George would be quite alright for another couple of hours. The vessel could be put about then, when they changed watches.

By seven a.m. however the wind had freshened considerably. It was time Arthur turned out. Putting the becket on the wheel, the mate ran forward as quickly as he could, for in the darkness he had to avoid the deck cargo. Leaning over the fore scuttle he bellowed down to the cook to turn out and come aft

Plate 21   *Clara May*
'The mate could see Arthur filling the kettle from the water tank.' The fresh water tank and copper dipper, with its lanyard, on board the ketch *Clara May*. Basil Greenhill

Left Plate 20   *Enid*
'The rattling of the heavy sheet blocks.' The mainsheet block of the ketch *Enid* at sea in 1939. The little *Enid*, built at Milford in 1903, has a much reduced rig as a motor ketch and is on short summer passages across the Bristol Channel. The end of the mainsheet is secured to the block in a most unseamanlike fashion. Such practices would not have been safe or tolerated in the *Mary Fletcher*. Gordon Mote

quickly. He had found the spray flying over the fore deck cold and unpleasant, the wind had actually increased as he ran forward, pushing the ship's bow up too close to the wind. That would happen, thought George as he scrabbled back to the wheel. Grabbing the wheel he quickly put the helm up. The old ship responded, but it was time to take some of the sail off her.

Arthur appeared within the limited range of light from the cabin skylight. 'Ship the handles on the reefing gear Art,' said George, 'main and mizzen. And get the falls off the pins ready for slacking away.'

Arthur, sensing the urgency in the mate's voice, quickly went forward to the mainmast to do as he was told. George, anxious not to appear too ready to shorten sail, was reluctant to call the Captain, for it was less than half an hour before he, the Captain, would have to turn out anyway. It was just beginning to get light now. The mate could see Arthur filling the kettle from the water tank (Plate 21) and the smoke that was pouring out of the galley flue pipe showed he had just replenished the fire. George thought of the Irish bacon that was probably by now in the pan.

As if the pleasure of daylight, which the spin of the earth had just brought to the people in the *Mary Fletcher* was resented by the elements, it now started to rain, a slanting driving rain, colder even than the east wind. Fortunately, however, George had just before caught sight of the North Lundy light bearing about a point of the lee bow.

Arthur ran aft to enquire about breakfast, but before he reached the companion way the Captain's head appeared. His first words was 'Did you pick up the light George before the rain came?' 'Yes, Cap'n', said the mate 'I saw the double flash just before the rain started, it was about a point off the starboard bow, but I never saw the loom of it. Must have been raining there I reckon.' They were of course talking about the North Lundy light. 'Can't be more than twelve miles off by the speed she's been going, but its flood tide—sweeping us up to windward, no need to worry about Lundy.' Then looking at Arthur he added 'More likely to make Bull Point on this course!!'

'Us could walk home from there!', said Arthur, whose home was only three miles from Bull Point. 'George', said Captain Trumper, 'I see you've everything ready; we'll put a couple of rolls in the main and the mizzen. This weather is not going to improve. The glass is still falling, and she'll be more comfortable then. It may save having to call you out too. But first we'll get the boom jib in.'

The two men, eager for their breakfast, wasted not a moment getting to the mainmast. Taking all the turns but one of the main throat halyard fall from its pin in the rail the mate surged the four inch rope allowing the jaws of the gaff to slide down the mast, thus slackening the luff of the sail. 'Wind her down Art, give it to her!', said George. Looking aft the mate saw the Captain holding up three fingers, meaning he had altered his mind and decided three rolls were necessary. Slacking away more of the throat halyard and making it fast, he then crossed the deck and slacked away on the peak halyard, made it fast, and went to the assistance of Arthur on the winding gear which was pretty ancient, and the wormed gear was badly worn (Plate 22).

Making sure the pawl was engaged, and securing the halyards and coiling the falls on the pins, the two men carried out the same operation on the mizzen. The whole reefing operation took less than ten minutes.

The vessel was steadier now, even though the wind seemed to be stronger, with less speed through the water the slamming of her bows was noticeably quieter. Breakfast would be somewhat late today. Arthur, before attending to the duties of the galley, had taken down the side lights and stern light, standing them in the galley ready to be filled and trimmed. The mate below in his room, looking in his mirror saw a grubby and unshaven face with two red-rimmed eyes staring out, the swollen lids adding ten years to his age. 'God above!!!' A darkening of the companion way. It was Arthur bringing the breakfast, in a dixie with a towel over it to keep out the rain.

'What's wrong this morning then Arthur?', said the mate. 'Why, its twenty past eight!!'. 'You must have put the clock on George', replied the cook, knowing he was being tantalized. He disappeared quickly up the ladder to

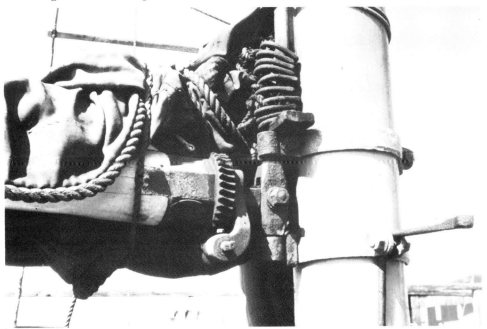

Plate 22   Reefing Gear
The *Mary Fletcher* was fitted with worm reefing gear of the type patented by George Williams of Appledore and manufactured by George and Alexander Beara of that place. She was given this gear in 1912 in place of the points reefing which had been used in vessels for centuries. The patent of the mizzen of the ketch *Emily Barrett*, built at Millom in 1913 and owned in Braunton, shows the helically cut gear on the boom which engaged with the worms underneath. The worms were turned with the handle, hanging from the mastband, which was put over the square end of the small shaft visible below the gear wheel. The *Emily Barrett*'s mizzen was jib headed, the weather of the sail lashed to hanks travelling on a track, instead of the normal mast hoops. Basil Greenhill

relieve the Captain at the wheel whilst George raked out the fore grate and pulled out the damper.

'Keep her as she's going Arthur', said Captain Trumper, 'S.E.E. it is, she's getting a bit wild,' 'Aye aye Cap'n', replied Arthur, knowing the compass card would be kept under observation and determined to do his best.

Down in the warm cabin as each man helped himself to his breakfast the Captain commented on the fact that they had had the wind on the port side from the time they left Kinsale Harbour. 'If we keep on this tack another hour' said the Captain, 'we may be lucky and weather the Helwick on the other.'

By the time George Cox had washed his face and got some of the grime off his hands it was nearly 9 a.m. In three hours he'd have to be at the helm again. The only sleep he'd had since heaving up the anchor twenty-six hours before in Kinsale Harbour was three and a half hours. Knowing that if he laid on the locker he would probably be thrown off when the ship was put about as the Captain intended, he spread his great coat on his bunk in his room to ensure—he hoped—the full three hours' sleep.

Meantime on deck the Captain estimated the wind was not far off force seven. If it increased any more he felt he might have to put the helm up. However, the flood tide must still be some help in pushing them farther to windward. He decided to let the ship run another half hour on the port tack. Lundy could not be more than five or six miles on the lee bow—if only the rain would let up. Visibility he thought was about a mile but with no objects as a guide he could not be sure.

At 10 a.m. Captain Trumper estimating that Lundy should now lie abeam, and as there could be no chance of hearing the fog siren with the wind as it was, decided to put the ship about. Calling to Arthur who was in the galley preparing the dinner he told him to stand by the jib sheet. Waiting until he thought he saw a smoother patch he called to the cook to 'Ease up!'

The jib sheet taut as a bar, surged around the bitt and the windlass end, the wet wood steaming with the friction; the rasping of the rope a warning to fumbling fingers.

At that same moment the Captain had put the helm down, and the *Mary Fletcher,* free of the restriction of the rudder a lee, free too of the restraint of the howling wind in the belly of the jib, flew up into the winds' eye as if leaping with joy, the chain part of the sheet flailing and slashing ready to mutilate the unwary, but of little concern to Arthur, a professional. But what leaps high usually has to come down and Arthur crossing over to secure the opposite sheet by a turn around the windlass end, felt as if his feet had left the deck, so sudden did the ship's bow dive into the trough of the sea. Suddenly the volume of water passing beneath the ship rose to the level of the top of the bulwarks around the bow, the pressure of water gushing in through both hawsepipes like two streams from two mighty hoses.

Arthur heard the crash of the main boom as it swung across and filled the sail.

The jib sheet now secure, he crossed the fore deck again and let draw the bowline of the staysail, the ship was around and on the starboard tack far quicker than it takes to write about it. The *Mary Fletcher* had been put through the wind at 10 a.m. on the second day of the passage, 26 hours out from Kinsale.

The mate, woken up by the crash of the mizzen boom as it flew across the deck and was brought up by its sheet on the opposite side, did not open his eyes, but turned over, wedged himself with his knees and promptly fell asleep again. Such things had happened many times before. Captain Trumper, with the vessel's head now looking N.N.E. and with the ebb tide running out at one and a half or two miles an hour could not expect much progress towards Cardiff, if any, before the next flood. If the ship would fetch near enough to Worms Head to gain the shelter of Rhossili Bay, they could probably dodge there under the weather shore until the next flood, otherwise it meant just sticking at it. In spite of the stronger wind, reefed down as she was, the *Mary Fletcher* was not making much over six knots. This told Captain Trumper it would take his ship four hours to make Rhossili Bay.

Arthur the cook, with the Captain's permission, was busily preparing an Irish stew for dinner. This was a favourite meal when they were experiencing inclement weather, for it could be prepared easily in one pot and, with the fiddle around the cooking range nothing could be upset. Furthermore a pot of stew with the lid on was easily transported to the cabin and stood on the fireplace there.

After the usual 'drill' with Arthur 'standing in' to take over the wheel whilst the Captain and the mate had their dinner in the cabin, the mate was once again at the helm. The Captain had said he would not undress and if he slept to be called at 1.30 p.m. Replete after a huge helping of Irish stew, followed by a mug of tea, George Cox would have dearly loved to turn into his bunk again. He knew the Welsh coast could not be much more than ten miles ahead, and the Helwick Lightship about six miles somewhere ahead, but on which bow? She may have held her own edging across the ebb tide; if she had, the light vessel would appear on the port bow. Had the tide, helped by the east wind, been that much stronger they might fetch to leeward.

If the weather would only clear! Still, thank God it was daylight, and Arthur the cook would keep an eye lifting. Must be half ebb now. Such were the thoughts of George Cox; weary from lack of sleep, cold and wet, his condition of mind and discomfort of body a medium for anxiety and doubt.

Arthur, having washed up the dinner dishes and cleaned out his pots, tidied the galley, made up the fire and came aft to the mizzen to try the port pump, but after a few strokes the pump sucked air showing that all was well. Walking back to the wheel he stood beside the mate saying, 'Let me take her George. Go and have a warm and a smoke in the galley.' 'Thanks, Art', said the mate, 'I'll do that; this rain makes a fellow feel colder than it is.' Then he added, 'It's one o'clock now, in another hour we should be nearing the Helwick. I shall want you up in the bows then Art. I can't see anything ahead with her in this trim.' 'Right-ho George', said the cook 'when you have had a fag and a warm. I'll get the lights up to the galley and prepare them ready to put up. 'Twill be dark before four in this weather.'

Later, back at the helm, George felt some puffs on the side of his face to windward. Looking aloft to the weft at the truck, rippling and gyrating across the sky with the rolling and tumbling of the ship, it was a job to judge in cold weather. Easing the helm he brought the vessel up to a point, no sign of a tremor in the luff of the mainsail. The ship's head was now N.E. by N. Easing the helm a bit more until the head was N.E. ½N, the trembling of the luffs told him it was too much. N.E.¾ was as much as she would do.

George took the time from the cabin clock, visible through the skylight, and chalked it down on his piece of asbestos. Nearly time to call the Captain anyway. In the boisterous weather such as the *Mary Fletcher* was experiencing, it was impossible to keep the 'lubbers line' on any given point of the compass to within a quarter of a point on either side of that line, for these vessels would swing a quarter point at least each way, each 'swing' correcting the opposite one (it was hoped!).

The mate felt more cheerful now, he estimated the vessel's head would be pointing up towards Port Eynon Point. Had the weather been clear he thought he would have been able to see the high land easily.

Meantime Arthur had put the three navigation lights ready, but unlit, in the galley and was up in the bows on the weather side wondering how far ahead he could see—he thought about a mile or even a mile and a half. Suddenly both Arthur and the mate heard the blast of a ship's fog siren somewhere to windward. The mate, loath to leave the wheel even for a few seconds with a steamship coming from 'God knows where', called to Arthur to 'come and give a blast on the fog horn.' The fog horn in the *Mary Fletcher* was a box about two feet long, by eighteen inches deep and nearly a foot wide and it could be carried like a suitcase. There was a handle outside (like the 'barrel organs' you can see in some folk museums) and evidently attached to the spindle was a series of gears, or cogs, and through these a fan was operated—at terrific speed—driving air past the reed of the horn. The bell of the horn protruded through the end of the box. The deep organ like note of that horn, in still and foggy weather, must have carried two miles. In boisterous conditions the sound range must have been limited, but in windy weather it was unlikely to be needed (Plate 23). The trouble always was, how far could one see!

George Cox knew the ship was now in the busy shipping lane between the upper Bristol Channel ports and the ports of south east Ireland and Liverpool, so he kept Arthur 'grinding away' at the fog horn at intervals of a minute. This

Right Plate 23   Foghorn
The *Mary Fletcher*'s foghorn was of the barrel organ type described in the text. Equally common was the bellows type, here shown on board the ketch *Clara May* in 1946. Basil Greenhill

brought the Captain's head up the companion way. The mate said 'Sorry if we woke you up Cap'n, but a steamboat blew not far away to windward, I thought we'd better play safe. Can't judge how far we can see.' 'You did quite right to play safe George,' said Captain Trumper, 'But if he'd been bound West you'd have seen him by now. Maybe somebody from around the land (Land's End) bound for Swansea, he'd have come up between Hartland and Lundy; maybe he saw somebody on the opposite course to himself. I reckon we can see nearly a mile, George, not much need to blow—but keep the "box" handy! The wind's gone a bit more southerly I see.'

'It's half past one o'clock Cap'n', said George, looking somewhat anxiously at the master. 'I know. George, I know!', replied the Captain, 'But we have three reefs in remember, and we can see more than a mile. Should have picked something up. I'll get my oilskins on.'

A few minutes later Arthur the cook with the sharp eyes of youth saw the buoy just off the starboard bow. Running aft to make himself heard the better he said 'looks like a chequered buoy—over a mile away.' Captain Trumper, by this time on deck, with the help of the mizzen shroud heaved himself up on to the gallant rail to enable him to look over the crests. 'You're right Arthur,' he said, looking his approval, 'It must be the Helwick swatch. There will be a lot of sea tumbling about around them today; give her another five minutes and we'll put her about.'

The Captain took the helm from George, who went forward to help Arthur. Came the familiar call 'Ease up!'. As George eased off the jib sheet, Arthur quickly took a loose turn around the starboard bitt and windlass end lest the wild monster—the jib—take control (Plate 24). It never failed to surprise them when the ship, freed of the restrictions of the helm, seemed to gambol up into the winds' eye in blusterous weather as if defying the very element that was her only highway. 'Watch out Art!' shouted George as the old ship, seeming to drop beneath their feet, twisted herself down into a trough; but the oncoming sea, in spite of the white water hissing down its slope, held no danger. True, it rose momentarily level, and above the rail, tumbling noisily aboard; George's shout was a warning to Arthur that they were going to get wet, no oilskins could be completely waterproof against such a deluge.

It was now nearly two o'clock. The *Mary Fletcher* was 30 hours out from Kinsale on the second day of the passage to Cardiff. George hurried back to the helm to let the Captain continue his watch below. Before Captain Trumper went below, however, he told the mate to stream the log. The ship's head was now S. by E.

Meantime Arthur—like a good 'cook' should—had nipped down to rake out the cabin fireplace and build up the fire before the Captain laid down on the cabin locker. Going on deck and standing by George at the helm, Arthur said, 'There'll be a dry towel in the galley by now George, why not go up and rub your head dry, take your oilskin off and dry your shoulders, you must have got wet same as I did. Have a fag in comfort too.'

Plate 24   *Bessie*
The windlass of the ketch *Bessie*, built at Milford in 1900 and owned in Braunton. The windlass levers have been shipped and the cable of the starboard anchor is lying slack around the drum. The vessel is moored alongside Velator Wharf. Despite the fact that the sails have not been unbent she is for sale. The starboard anchor, which has been laid out in the stream, will be used to pull her head off from the quay when she moves away. Note also that the starboard link rod connecting the crosshead with the starboard bellows of the windlass has been unshipped, presumably to prevent children turning the windlass. The *Bessie* was sold to Mediterranean owners in 1946 and was lost in the Red Sea. Basil Greenhill

'Her head's south by east, Art, just about pointing straight to Ilfracombe! But with the ebb running out we'll be lucky to fetch above Morte Point.' Stepping away from the wheel the mate added: 'Thanks, Art, you could almost be a Somerset man!' Stepping quietly down the cabin companionway he snatched a spare Appledore jersey off its peg, noted the Captain was already asleep, and quickly made his way to the galley. Removing the sticky and cheerless oilskin coat, his reefer jacket and jersey, he rubbed the salty dampness from his neck and shoulders and put on the dry, thick and heavy Appledore knitted jersey (Plate 25). The shirt had to stay: that would soon dry out. No one ever caught cold with salt water—it was being cold that sapped a man's will.

The mate could have changed his clothes down in his own room, but the crackling of the oilskins would have awakened the Captain and in those little vessels the tiny overworked crews had to consider each other. This the majority of them did, and the result was harmony.

At four p.m. Captain Trumper took over the helm. When the log was hauled in

the reading was nearly twelve miles. The thick and rumbustuous weather, rarely experienced together, was depressing. It was only thirty-two hours since they streamed the log off Kinsale, but it felt like a week. The Bull Point light could be only about nine miles ahead. In thick quiet weather fog sirens could be heard for miles. But with the wind as it was, and the turbulent sea, sounding its noisy anger, no other sounds could hope to compete against such odds. Captain Trumper felt cut off. One grain of comfort was that as they neared Bull Point there would be some shelter from the high land with the wind making slightly off shore. This should quieten the sea.

It was now nearly five o'clock and the Captain had decided to play safe and put the vessel about, when Arthur, keeping a lookout up in the bows, shouted back that he could see the loom of a flashing light off the port bow. Calling Arthur back to the helm, Captain Trumper went forward himself. Sure enough well away on the port bow was the loom of a quick flashing light every ten seconds—it must be the Bull, and the ebb tide had taken them to leeward more than expected.

This cheered the Captain up, nothing to worry about now. With the light beaming as it was he could safely keep going, for the *Mary Fletcher*'s bow must be pointing into Bideford Bay, and with the easterly wind he would be under a weather shore. Furthermore they would be down wind of the mighty fog siren of the Bull, they'd probably hear that too. Getting on for low water as well!

Back on the quarter deck with Arthur, the Captain told him to put the kettle on ready for a hot drink later on, and then to watch out for a red light—or the loom of a red fixed light from the same direction as the white flasher. 'As soon as we see that, Arthur', said the Captain, 'We'll put her on the other tack, and have a cup of something to warm us up.'

Before long came a call from Arthur saying he could see a faint red glow, and a few moments later Captain Trumper saw it himself, a stronger glow but not the light itself. He knew then they were within the arc of the fixed red light of the Bull. The sea suddenly became less turbulent, the weight of the wind decidedly quieter—the *Mary Fletcher* was in the lee of the high coast of Devon. Came the familiar call 'Ease up!'; no flogging sheets or 'stomach lifting' downward plunges this time, the change from the motion and noise was like a calm.

Arthur heard it first—a high pitched reedy blast, sounding eerie and remote, the Bull fog siren coming down wind. Captain Trumper heard it the second time.

Left Plate 25   Appledore Quay
Appledore quay before it was widened in 1940. The ketches off the quay include the *Francis Beddoe*, built at Saundersfoot in 1877, and the *Humility*, mid foreground, built at Littlehampton in 1838 between them, further upstream, is the *Julia*, built at Bideford in 1876. Lying off the quay upstream of the *Humility* is the *Nellie Mary*, built at Plymouth in 1882. All these vessels were owned in Appledore. The man on the left is Captain Thomas Powe of the *Humility*. Standing on the planks is Captain William Schiller, master of the ketch *Lively*. Both men are wearing the Appledore jerseys of the type George Cox put on after his soaking when the *Mary Fletcher* was put through the wind. From an old Postcard

Calling to the cook he said, 'Before you make the tea Arthur try the pump while she's more on an even keel.' But Arthur only managed to pump out a few strokes, the old ship had made no water.

The term cook, I fear, may be somewhat misleading when used to refer to Arthur Ferryman, who, the reader will have noticed, could take the helm when called upon, help put the ship about, etc, for, of course, Arthur was a very competent seaman. With only three hands aboard he had to be. Arthur Ferryman carried out the duties of the galley because he was the most appropriate person available—it was an added duty some one was forced to do in the lean times of that period. A sixteen-year-old lad could be the 'cook', or an aged ship's mate who had got beyond the more strenuous duties of the ship—if the extra hand could be afforded! Any girl who married a man who had spent some years in such vessels as the *Mary Fletcher,* nine times out of ten married a fairly competent cook. Wise men however did not usually advertise that ability.

Away now on the starboard tack, her head pointing N.E. by N. it was 5.30 p.m. and just about low water. As they lost the loom of the fixed red light of the Bull Point Captain Trumper re-set and streamed the log. The course they were steering would bring them a mile or so westward of the Scarweather lightvessel—less than twenty miles ahead. But with the flood tide now under their lee, the three hours' run (if the wind held) should put them four miles to windward—that is up Channel— of the Scarweather at least.

The *Mary Fletcher,* now leaving the comforting lee of the land, felt the full force of the wind again. However it had eased a little, but the tide, now flowing to windward, made the seas more steep and consequently more uncomfortable.

By eight o'clock that evening, on the second day from Kinsale after 36 hours at sea, with the flood 2½ hours gone and the next high water due at 12 o'clock midnight, 40 hours out of Kinsale, they picked up the flashing light of the Scarweather Lightship, but it was only a blurred light, for if anything the visibility was worse than before. Captain Trumper judged the light to be about two or three miles off the port bow.

They were in the busy steamer track and for the last half hour Arthur had been 'winding out' one blast every minute on the fog horn, Now, as soon as the mate appeared on deck to start his watch, the Captain decided to put the vessel about, for should the wind die away it would be better for the ship to be well off in the channel than inside a line from Scarweather to the Nash. This was a great relief to George the mate, it meant he would have the whole watch with open water ahead of him at the speed they were going and, hopefully, not much traffic to bother about. It would also, as they would be on the port tack, now be necessary to give two blasts on the foghorn instead of one. The ship's head was now S.S.E. but within the next hour the wind had veered a little and lost some of its strength. The sea went down too, and with it the lively motion of the ship was reduced accordingly.

George felt it was time to shake out the reefs, but to play safe decided to leave it for another half hour. Arthur had taken the foghorn up on the forward hatchway, the farthest convenient spot from the cabin aft where the blasts were not so likely to keep the Captain awake.

At 9.30 p.m. the mate called to Arthur to release the pawl from the ratchet of the main reefing gear, and take the throat halyards off the pin. Immediately this was done George put the becket on the wheel and ran forward to help 'swig' up the luff of the sail. This accomplished, the mate ran back to the wheel again, steadied the little ship up again, for she had wandered a point off course, and waited for Arthur to call for the final 'swig up' on the peak halyards. When this came it was the same drill as before, for no man could set the *Mary Fletcher*'s mainsail up as taut as it should be without help from a second man, or by putting a turn around the lower barrel of the dolly winch. Even then it was not a job to be envied in the dark, especially on that particular trip when the decks were cluttered with deck cargo.

Setting up the mizzen was a job one man could manage. In any case the helmsman was near enough to give a hand if necessary.

Time now—10 p.m.—for Arthur to brew a cup of cocoa for the man at the wheel—and one for himself of course. In clear weather, and in more open water, after the 10 o'clock brew it was usual for the cook to be more or less 'off duty'. In the circumstances that prevailed that night aboard the *Mary Fletcher,* however, the fickle wind, and the very murky weather that enveloped the ship, for the third hand to leave the deck, except for a minute or two, would be unthinkable, especially with a fog horn that was worked by winding a handle. A fog horn that was sounded by a man blowing into it could be blown by the helmsman. The unfortunate third hand therefore was bound by a code of practice for which the only alternative was a *fourth hand.* Yet a fourth hand could, if quick passage could not be achieved, make all the difference between profit and loss. Such were the conditions crews were forced to endure in vessels the owners could not afford to lay up and would have been unable to sell—even had they wanted to—because they could not compete with the rapidly increasing numbers of motor craft which could make three times as many passages in the same time and run to timetables more attractive to the ship brokers.

But Arthur Ferryman did not think of these problems of economics. He could foresee he was going to be on deck until the Captain came on watch at midnight and, should the weather not clear, during the next watch as well. The foghorn was bound to be kept going, and the 'shuffley' (fickle) wind might bring a call at any moment to trim the sails.

The *Mary Fletcher* had now been on the port tack two hours. After drinking their cocoa the mate told Arthur to haul in and read the log. The reading showed the ship had only covered nine miles in the two hours—nine miles through the water, the flood tide was also sweeping her to the eastward towards her destination. This put them about five miles off the Somerset coast,'Anyway, we're well above the Foreland,' thought the mate. The light must be somewhere off the starboard bow. After Arthur had streamed the log and made up his galley fire, likewise the forecastle fire—each chore being interrupted every minute (or there about) to wind out two blasts on the foghorn—he went aft to the mate saying: 'Shall I take her for a bit George to give you a spell?', and George having been standing there for nearly two and a half hours, was glad of the chance to stretch his legs even though it meant having the chore of the mournful sounding foghorn.

They both heard and felt it together—a bump and a jar under the counter. It was the heavy rudder sliding up and down on its worn pintles as the stern rose and sank with the heave and fall of the sea. It was a certain sign that the vessel had lost most of her way, thus allowing the rudder to jump up and down unrestrained through lack of friction through the water. Simultaneously the two booms swung inboard, there being no wind to keep them steady.

George quickly took in all the slack of the main sheet to keep the boom from flailing about, whilst Arthur hauled in the mizzen. With no wind in her sails to steady the old ship, what bit of billow there was caused her to tumble about in every direction but the one expected.

Then away to the eastward Arthur Ferryman, again with the keen eyes of youth, saw a flash, a single flash. Fearing he might be mistaken he kept looking in the same direction. After what seemed a long interval he saw it again. Calling to George, he scrabbled aft over the deck cargo and pointed to where, as he thought, he had seen the flashes; but the *Mary Fletcher* out of control with no way on her, was by then pointing in quite a different direction, so they missed the next flash. The mate standing ready by the binnacle casting quick glances at the compass card whilst watching for the flash to the eastward saw the sudden tiny burst of hazy light at the same time as Arthur. Taking a rough bearing by the simple method of placing his outstretched hand across the face of the compass, he judged the light to be bearing E. by N. 'Start counting the seconds next time you see it Arthur, while I watch the compass and point out the bearing for you.' They both saw the next feeble flash and Arthur counted to 13 before they glimpsed the next one. There were actually 15 second intervals between flashes.

'That must be the Breaksea Lightship', said a deep voice from the cabin scuttle. It was the Captain standing on the stairs of the companion way. 'You'm awake then Cap'n!', said Arthur. 'Who could sleep in this tumble', replied the Captain. 'The play on that rudder would wake a dead man! Have to get it seen to I suppose.'

Just when the mate saw another light over the stern—a white light. Suddenly it disappeared, starting to count the seconds, before he reached four the light appeared again. 'Must be the Nash', said the mate. Captain Trumper disappeared below but only for a few minutes. Reappearing he said, 'It's the Nash alright, I got a good fix. We're about 6 miles off the Nash and a bit less than 9 miles below Breaksea. The tide is pushing us up channel nearly three knots an hour.'

By now it was 11 p.m. The *Mary Fletcher* was 39 hours out of Kinsale and it was about an hour to high water. George felt an air of wind from the eastward, or may be it was just the movement the ketch was given by the tidal current causing the faint breeze to fill the sails and give her bare steerage way. The irritating bumps of the rudder had nearly ceased and George prevailed upon Captain Trumper to go and lie down again. 'I'll do that then', said the Captain, 'But watch the bearings of the light George, for fear the murk comes down again.' 'That I will Cap'n, you know that!', replied the mate. Arthur said to George, ' 'Tis a God send not to have to wind up that bloody fog horn!!'

There was no change in the weather when the Captain took over at midnight. The murky conditions still prevailed, with hardly enough wind to give the vessel any steerage way. Soon it would be high water, and any hope of being able to make the Somerset shore and anchor in either Porlock or Lynmouth bay whilst the ebb ran out was nil. Captain Trumper now had the deck to himself. Before the two men had gone below to lie on their respective lockers he had helped them set the gaff topsail. Although there was now no breeze from any direction, the Captain knew that as soon as the ebb started to run to the westward at its maximum speed (which, he knew, in these parts was about 2¼ miles an hour on an average spring tide) sweeping the vessel back over the ground she had so laboriously gained on the flood, that in itself would create a 'false' air of wind enough to fill the sails and so give the ship enough steerage to keep her head up channel and so very considerably slow her sternway over the ground.

By the end of his watch, that is, at 4 a.m. when the *Mary Fletcher* was 44 hours out of Kinsale, the Captain reckoned that, according to the bearing of the Nash which he could still dimly see, the *Mary Fletcher* had lost about six miles to the westwards, showing that the air of wind created by the ebb had saved about four miles. As George the mate remarked when he took over from Captain Trumper, 'That old tops'el certainly helped her stem the tide.' Just after the Captain went below George, looking astern, saw what he thought were the four white flashes of the Foreland lighthouse. Later he saw it quite a few times: shrouded in the persistent haze it looked vague and remote. Fearing the fog might return he took a hasty bearing, it was W. by S. He then took a bearing of the Nash, it was N. by E. He chalked these two bearings on his asbestos slate together with the time they were taken. Should the fog return he would go down to the cabin, risking waking the Captain, and mark the bearings off the chart, thereby ensuring a spot from which to calculate.

This method of fixing a vessel's position is laughable when compared with today's modern instruments for navigation. Yet those old methods served their purpose in the little coasting vessels; it was rare for one of them to be lost through an error of navigation. At low water, just after 6 a.m., much the same conditions prevailed. Dawn was in the eastern sky, paling the lights of the Foreland and the Nash yet failing to reveal the outlines of the coasts on either side. At 6.30 a.m., just after low water, the mate took the bearings of the last faint glimmers of the two lighthouses. The Foreland was bearing S.W. ½W, the Nash N.E. ½E. After this the lights could not be seen at all, neither did full daylight show any sign of the land. George knew that high water at Cardiff would be at approximately 1.30 p.m., if they made it this would be 53½ hours out of Kinsale. George entered the bearings on his slate. They would be a good help if the really thick weather returned.

It was time now to call Arthur out of his bunk. The first of the flood was now making itself felt, creating for the *Mary Fletcher* as she was carried along, a faint air of wind now from the east. This allowed the old ship to be kept broadside to the stream on either tack thus gaining all the benefit there was from the power of the current.

Arthur, coming on deck, his face puffed up with sleep, went first to the galley to stir the fire and put the kettle on, next he took down the navigation lights, by which time the kettle was boiling. Pouring the water on the inevitable cocoa he carried his own cup aft, stood it on the skylight, and took the wheel from the mate, 'Get up and have a warm George', he said.'What's the course anyway?' 'There aint one!', said George: 'It's only the tide giving us an air. Just try and keep her sails full'. 'I notice we're still on the port tack!' said Arthur, looking accusingly at George but with a smile in his eyes.

By 8 a.m., when they were 48 hours out of Kinsale, the wind came from the east. It was only a light breeze but, coupled with the flood tide under her lee, the

Plate 26   *Mary Stewart*
The iron ketch *Mary Stewart*, built on the Clyde in 1876, off the North Devon coast near the border with Somerset, just west of the landfall made by the *Mary Fletcher*. In 1927, when this photograph was taken, the vessel was owned in Ilfracombe and had an auxiliary engine and reduced main topmast and jibboom. Basil Greenhill

Mary Fletcher heeled and drew ahead, causing a musical ripple under her counter as her stern slipped through the water, leaving a string of whirlpools in her lengthening wake.

The Captain, having had his breakfast of Irish bacon and eggs, served by the cook, came on deck. The easterly breeze had brought with it miserable mist, half rain, half fog. He played safe and ruled off the bearings the mate had taken at dawn and, as the vessel had been without a breeze for most of the time, allowance for drift with the tidal stream was all that was necessary.

With the vessel's head pointing S.E. by S. and the tide under her lee Captain Trumper expected to pick up the land somewhere above Minehead (Plate 26). The wind was freshening, and in just over an hour, at 9.45 a.m., Arthur saw what they thought was the high land of North Hill.

Abreast of Minehead the Captain and Arthur put the vessel about onto the starboard tack. It was now 10.15 a.m. and, as the wind had suddenly increased, whilst the vessel was in stays the two men ran the topsail down and stowed it at the foot of the mast. The sky to the eastward had now grown dark, and as the rain increased so did the growl of the wind in the rigging aloft and alow. Just before twelve noon they heard the shrill penetrating sound of the fog signal from the Breaksea Lightship not far off the starboard bow, showing how the flood tide had pushed the old ship up to windward. Just as the mate came on deck to relieve the Captain the easterly wind–true to form–suddenly increased in force, lying the ship over and sending some of the top logs of the deck cargo down to leeward. The Captain, concerned that something aloft might carry away, eased the helm, letting the vessel come up near the wind. At the same time he gestured to George and Arthur to wind down a roll in the mainsail. The two men needed no telling. The mate cast off the main throat halyards and, in a few seconds, lowered away the jaws of the gaff, whilst Arthur shipped the winch handle and wound down two rolls of the boom. Next they ran back to the mizzen and speedily put two rolls in that sail as well.

Whilst they were doing this the mate, puffing from his exertions, caught the Captain's eye and said, 'The boom jib Cap'n?' 'As quick as you can George', said the Captain, 'Just haul it down and make the down-haul fast, then we'll put her about as smartly as we can–must be pretty near the shore,' As the jib ran down the stay, slamming and thundering, the two men saw the land looming through the driving rain, they thought about three cables away. 'Ready about!', came the call from aft. This was the manoeuvre old Georgie Morgan, walking on the shore looking for driftwood, had observed at the start of this story.

Abreast of Penarth Pier the two men slacked the bobstay off the windlass, eased the shank chain and levered the bill of the anchor off the rail. The wind had suddenly eased, due most likely to the mighty bulk of Penarth Head causing an eddy and bringing pause to its flow (Plate 27). As the *Mary Fletcher* swept past the Inner Wrack buoy, Arthur slacked away the shank chain of the anchor, leaving it to swing hanging ready at the cat-head, George the mate overhauling

Plate 27 *Irene*
The ketch *Irene*, built at Bridgwater in 1907, under mainsail and auxiliary motor, dipping into a ground sea off Nash Point in May 1959. The *Irene* was the last westcountry trading ketch to work carrying cargoes. She is still afloat, now fully rigged again, as a cruise and charter vessel. Captain William Schiller

Plate 28 *Kathleen & May*
The gaskets have been placed on the foreboom and the first is being put into position on the main, preparatory to taking in sail. Note the mast hoops, and that the foot of the sails are secured to jackstays on the booms because the vessel has roller reefing gear on all her three masts. Note also the deck cargo, covered with a tarpaulin, on the after hatch—the seaman is standing on it—and the boat secured on the fore hatch, also the galley abaft the foremast with the galley chimney on the starboard side. Basil Greenhill

a few fathoms of chain. Clear of the mouth of Ely Harbour Captain Trumper put the helm down, rounded the vessel up head to wind and, as soon as she lost way there came the call 'let go!'. They had just made it. It was 2 p.m., twenty minutes past high water, and the passage from Kinsale had taken 54 hours.

The crew had hardly finished stowing the sails (Plate 28)–stiff as boards owing to the never ending rain–when the inevitable tug arrived. The master told them the merchants had been expecting them the day before! 'I can take you straight into the berth now if you like', he told Captain Trumper.

Although the crew of the *Mary Fletcher* were wet, weary and hungry, and had been looking forward to their dinner in peace and comfort, Captain Trumper could not refuse such an offer of quick service, with the added prospect even, of starting discharging that same day. 'We shall have to give you a five inch warp' said Captain Trumper, addressing the tug master, 'we haven't launched the boat, as you can see.' In most sailing coasters of that time the eight inch or ten inch towing hawser was coiled down like a huge Catherine wheel on the main hatchway and the lifeboat stowed on top of it when the vessels were at sea. 'Fair enough', said the tug master, 'we'll have you in and tied up in half an hour.'

Meantime the mate had gestured to Arthur to go forward with him and the two of them shipped the windlass levers and started to heave in the anchor chain (Plate 29), whilst the Captain put the eye of the warp aboard the tug and passed the bight of the warp in the forward chock.

The master of the tug, manoeuvring his vessel with the dexterity of forty years' practice, took the strain on the warp as the cable was 'up and down', thus breaking out the anchor from its bed in the Cardiff clay and saving the two men the hardest heaving of all. 'Thanks skipper', called the mate. The tug gave an answering 'toot' and proceeded slowly ahead to enable the anchor to be hove up to the foretoot without too much exertion (Plate 30). This accomplished, and the heavy six foot iron levers unshipped and stowed away, the two crew got the fenders over the side in readiness for when they entered the lock. Next they took the gripes off the boat (Plate 31) and hooked on the burtons fore and aft ready to lift her over the side when the vessel reached the discharging berth.

All this was done without a word from Captain Trumper. There was no need of words, it was routine, the never-ending graft necessary in all such vessels as the *Mary Fletcher*. Time now to get the mooring ropes ready for when they entered the lock.

One short sharp blast from the tugboat's siren told them the tugmaster had been signalled to keep to the starboard side of the lock. Said the mate to Arthur, 'In a couple of minutes Art they'll be aiming the heaving lines at us and bawling for the warps, good time now to see if the dinner's all burnt up!' But at that moment a 'toot toot' came from the tug and a wave of a hand from her wheelhouse. It was the signal to shorten in the tow warp before entering the lock.

The crew had their dinner that evening after the *Mary Fletcher* was tied up in

Plate 30   *Thomas Edwin*
A ketch, light, that is without cargo, under tow in the Bristol Channel. She is believed to be the
Thomas Edwin, built at Gunnislake, Cornwall, in 1867 and owned in Appledore. She has just picked
up the tug and the crew are busy stowing the mainsail. The head sails have been hauled down and are
hanging on the stays. The mizzen is still set. The starboard anchor is at the hawse pipe, the port
anchor on the rail. James Randall

Left Plate 29   *Clara May*
At work at the windlass of the ketch *Clara May*, owned in Braunton. The starboard anchor has just
been broken out and brought up to the hawse pipe for a short passage in sheltered water. Captain
Parkhouse is stowing a windlass lever. Basil Greenhill

her discharging berth, and after they had taken the lashings off the deck cargo and launched the boat over the side. The two latter chores were done to enable them to have an hour longer in their bunks the following morning.

The one blessing the charter gave them, for once, was a 'free discharge', that is, the cargo was not handled by the crew but by shore labour.

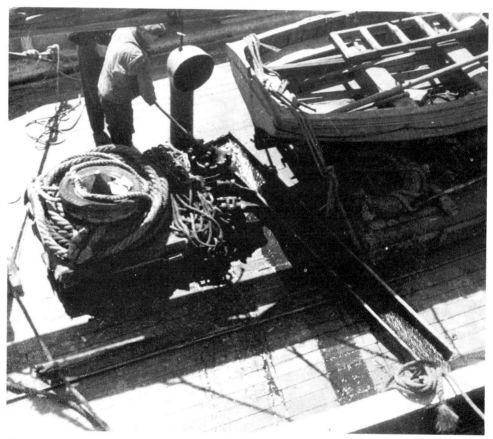

Plate 31   *Emma Louise*
The gripes are still firmly on this boat, securing her on the mainhatch. The vessel, the ketch *Emma Louise*, has just arrived at Minehead on the Somerset coast from Lydney with a cargo of coal and is being pumped out. Unlike the *Mary Fletcher*, fifty-five years old, which gave Arthur very little work at the pump, she made so little water, the *Emma Louise*, sixty-five years old when this photograph was taken in 1946, has taken in a lot even on a short passage in sheltered water. Basil Greenhill

CHAPTER 4

The next day Captain Trumper returned from the ship broker's office with the news that he had been offered a cargo of coal from Newport to the River Yeo. 'I didn't give an answer straight away George', he told the mate, 'I've never been there; thought I'd have a word with you first. I've heard you talk of it.'

'I was born not far from the pier,' said George, 'But I can't understand them offering you a cargo. The only vessels that ever traded into that river are the two owned by the railway company—the *Sarah* and the *Lily* (Plate 32), and I've sailed in both,* 'What about depth of water, George? What did *Sarah* draw?' 'She drew about ten feet, but you needn't worry, there's plenty of water for us. Easy enough to drop up the river with the anchor down should the wind be contrary', answered George. The Captain said 'There's no sounding anywhere near the mouth of the river shown on my chart, is it all mud flats thereabout?' 'Cap'n,' said George, 'there's nought to worry about at all. When I joined the *Sarah* she had a new skipper who had never been into the Yeo. We had no trouble, I know every yard of those mud flats. My father and I stuck a sixteen foot sapling on the best lead in over the bar. It had some twigs on the top, we called it "bushy stick". It's probably still there; there's a cross bar nailed to it ten foot up.'

The Captain, reassured, made the short journey to the Brokers and fixed for the cargo from Newport river to the Yeo, the crew to discharge the ship under the crane at the railway company's wharf on the west bank of the Yeo. The freightage was 2/2d per ton, or 11 new pence, bringing total freight for the *Mary Fletcher*'s cargo of 130 tons to just over £14.00.

Leaving Cardiff at approximately 4 a.m. on the early morning tide the day

---

*The trow *Sarah* and the ketch *Lily* were both real vessels which traded to the River Yeo. The *Sarah* was built at Framilode, Gloucestershire, in 1873, 43 tons net, 78 feet long. The *Lily* built at Penryn, Cornwall, in 1897, 25 tons, was only 56 feet long. The author sailed in both these vessels and was for some time master of the *Lily*.

after the pitprops were discharged, a light northerly wind took them off to Cardiff Roads, where they anchored whilst the ebb ran out. Low water in Cardiff Roads was at 10 a.m.

On the first of the flood the *Mary Fletcher* proceeded on her way, a very light westerly breeze making it necessary for her to have her topsail set even for that short distance—about 8 miles—to the mouth of the River Usk; without the topsail she would have had very little steerage way.

However, before half tide she was into the mouth of the river and, hauling her wind, sailed in past the dock entrance before any outbound traffic was about to cause anxiety to her master. No comfortable berth beside a wall in the still waters of the dock for the *Mary Fletcher;* she was to load her cargo at the jetties on the west bank of the river where the tide ran pretty strong on the flood, but much more swiftly on the ebb. With a rise and fall from 25 and 30 feet this meant constant attention to the mooring ropes. Nevertheless the saving in dock dues was very gratifying considering the miserly freight. Gratifying to the master and part owner, that is. With just enough wind in the topsail to give her steerage way, the old ship, with her anchor down to her forefoot ready to let go, sailed within a cable's length of the jetties (Plate 33). There the crew ran all her sails down, dropped her anchor on the bottom, the *Mary Fletcher* swung head to stream. They let her drag her anchor slowly with the stream until she was opposite her berth by the jetties, then the Captain sheered her in, bringing her in beside the piles with hardly a jar to be felt. With the lightest of winds, together with the use of the tide and the skill of her crew, the *Mary Fletcher* was ready to load at 3 p.m., five hours after leaving Cardiff roads. A heaving line came snaking down from the quay: 'Bend a bowrope on George,' shouted the lilting voice of a man with a black face. The mate, bending the line to the four inch rope in about two seconds, called out 'Thanks Taffy, I know your voice, can't place you with that make-up on!'. Another dark face peered down from above the stern, calling for the stern rope, and another heaving line was thrown down.

Arthur, who as soon as the anchor was down had put some salt cod in the cooking pot for a quick dinner immediately the ship was tied up, realising something was afoot, called up to a third man who had now appeared 'What's up you fellows? You gone mad or something?' 'No more than usual!', said the third man, 'but your coal's here and we can load you whilst the tide's high and you're close up to the chutes!'.

Captain Trumper, who had been in the cabin and had heard these verbal exchanges, quickly popped up asking if he had 'heard aright'. 'Yes Cap'n,' said the foreman, 'Twelve trucks have been here for three days. It was the cargo for

Left Plate 32   Three Vessels in Ilfracombe
The rugged coast at North Devon has few harbours. Here two old vessels, the smack *Mary*, built at Chepstow in 1817, and the ketch *Three Sisters*, built at Cowes in 1800 and no doubt much rebuilt, together with the much newer ketch *Lily* (see text) lie on the beach at Ilfracombe in the early 1920s. The *Three Sisters* is discharging into carts. From an old Postcard

the *Sarah* for the River Yeo. Two days ago came the news she had been in collision somewhere up channel and lost her rudder. We had a phone call yesterday telling us you had been chartered and the thirteenth truck came down this morning—making it up to 130 tons.' The Captain looking at George the mate said, 'That answers your question of yesterday when you said, "What's happened to the *Sarah* then?" '

The four coal trimmers, who were piece work men, that is, paid by results, quickly opened up the hatchways and stacked the hatches, whilst the crew slacked off the main boom and secured it clear of the hatch. Time only for a rough tie up of the sails, and to put on their canvas coats to keep the dust that would soon envelope the ship in a cloud of carbon black from destroying the whiteness of the canvas.

It was 5 p.m. and high water before the whine of the hydraulic lift gave notice that the first truck was being upended into the chute. 'Stand from under!', came the call as the door of the hatch was opened, only partly at first, to allow for a 'build up' of a few tons on the ship's inner skin to prevent damage to the planking. The second truck showed no mercy, it came down like a landslide causing the little ship to plunge down to 'leeward' as though in a seaway, no eyes could see through the bank of dust that lifted skywards as if from an explosion. It darkened the sky and clung to everything with the tenacity of face powder on a greasy skin. Four more trucks emptied their loads into the main hatch in quick succession. Then a slight pause whilst the ship was winched ahead fifteen or twenty feet to bring the after hatch, only three feet square, beneath the chute. Two more truck loads, or maybe three, went down that tiny hatch (Plate 34); the four trimmers now started furiously trimming, i.e., shovelling, the pinnacle of small lumps as it quickly built up under the narrow hatchway, rendering the dust laden hold a dark and stifling cave where every corner had to be filled to deck level if the ship was to load her full 130 tons. Soon, as the cargo built up, it became necessary for the trimmers each to produce a candle, which was lit and stood on the most convenient ledge, so that each man could see any pockets which may have been missed when shovelling back through the swirling dust. That was most important, otherwise when the ship was full she would not be down to her Plimsoll line and the Captain would know she had not been properly trimmed. If a train load of coal had been standing in heavy rain for a couple of days a ship could be down to her loaded marks before she was full.

Unpleasant as it was trimming and filling the hold to deck level around the tiny after hatch, the work forward of the main hatch was heavier, even though

Left Plate 33 *Martin Luther*
'With just enough wind in the topsail to give her steerage way, the old ship, with her anchor down to her forefoot ready to go, sailed within a cable's length of the jetties.' The ketch *Martin Luther*, built at Cowes in 1847, a smaller vessel than the *Mary Fletcher* but like the *Mary Fletcher*, with a boom on her staysail and a whale back lavatory shelter, in her case in the way of the starboard mizzen rigging, is shown in this photograph performing a similar manoeuvre in the Bridgwater River in Somerset. W. A. Sharman

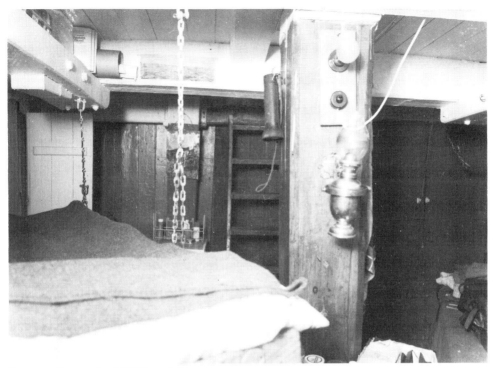

Plate 35   Forecastle of *Kathleen & May*
Arthur went 'to his lonely berth in the forecastle'. The forecastle of *Kathleen & May* when she was a working vessel. Basil Greenhill

there was more room to move. There the ship was at her widest, and the forward bulkhead was ten feet from the fore end of the hatchway. George the mate and Arthur had quickly battened down the after hatch. George said, 'Art, 'tis a good job the rules make it compulsory for the shore men to do the trimming. It's a wonder they haven't tried that out on us—we have to trim the oats we load in Ireland!'. 'If ever it comes to that', said Arthur, 'I shall leave the vessels for good. Don't forget the crews shovel out most cargoes of coal, I would never slave away like those poor sods down below there at this minute!' The 'poor sods' as Arthur called them were coming up from the hold seemingly glad to be able to stretch their legs and backs upright. They sat on the bulwarks wiping their sweating faces, the arc lights—or clusters suspended over the tipping gear and chute brought out their lined features in sharp relief. The crew made good use of the bright lights from above to heave plenty of water around to get rid of most of the coal dust. Even Captain Trumper, anxious to keep his cabin clean, did his

Left Plate 34   *Progress*
The Bideford ketch *Progress*, built at Kingsbridge in 1884, loading coal under the chutes at Lydney Dock in 1936. Her main hatch has been run full, she has been winched astern fifteen or twenty feet and the contents of the next truck are being tipped down the forehatch. After another truckload or two the trimmers will start work in the hold. Note the whaleback wheel shelter and the white panelled galley on deck. Basil Greenhill

share of the washing down, from the taffrail to the mizzen mast. In an hour the *Mary Fletcher,* battened down and her decks clear of the dust and grit, could wait till the next flood and daylight. Then they could make her properly free from the grime which only the broad light of day would reveal on every ledge and in every crevice.

High supper in the cabin that night, gammon rashers and two fried eggs each, and big Irish potatoes baked in the galley over. This was a concession owing to the mid-day meal being interrupted by the zeal of the shippers to start the loading almost before the vessel was tied up. Tea time had been a failure too because no one wanted to open up the cabin or the forecastle—the scuttles of both were sealed by canvas covers—before the main of the dust and grit had been cleared away. Now, however, cleaned and replete and dropping with tiredness, the three men sought their bunks. The Captain and the mate to their respective rooms and Arthur to his lonely berth in the forecastle (Plate 35).

At slack tide the next morning just before high water at approximately 6 a.m. with all the mooring ropes aboard except a slip rope, they hoisted the head of the standing jib. The wind being westerly, at dead high water that tiny bit of sail was sufficient, when the slip rope was hauled in, to blow the old ship with her 130 tons of coal in her hold off to mid-stream where the anchor was let go ready to drop the ship astern downstream with the anchor acting as a drogue. This was the only way when the wind was foul to get to the river's mouth. But it was a simple and effective way.

It was nearly two miles to the mouth of the river, an hour and a half of anchor drill whilst the Captain steered his ship stern first. Nevertheless each man managed to enjoy a cold breakfast as they took turn about. Once clear of Fifoots point the mainsail was set, the anchor hove clear of the bottom and, as she canted, two jibs were hauled up, the main sheet hauled hard in, next the mizzen was set, then the staysail. With the tide as it was running to windward at about four miles per hour, the *Mary Fletcher* was finding plenty of wind, but the mate suggested to Captain Trumper that if they wanted to get inside St Thomas's Head while there was plenty of water to accommodate the *Mary Fletcher*'s eleven foot draught it would be good policy to set the topsail. 'Otherwise', said George, 'we shall have to go below Sand Point and dodge about till the flood tide makes.'

Looking to the westward where the sky looked somewhat wild Captain Trumper decided to take the mate's advice. Bending on the halyard and sheet the two men hoisted the topsail aloft. While the Captain luffed his vessel into the eye of the wind to prevent the flogging topsail from filling, otherwise ten men could not have hauled it up, let alone two. The *Mary Fletcher* was really thrashing through the water now, her lee gunwale awash, and heavy spray flying aboard over her weather bow. Captain Trumper was finding it hard work to prevent her from luffing up, the vessel wanted so much weather helm. This meant she was not balanced, the answer would have been to set the flying jib, but that with the topsail set could have sprung the topmast.

Soon the vessel was clear of the West Middle Ground sand, with the English and Welsh Grounds lightship on her starboard hand. She was finding the full force of the ebb now running out of the Severn sweeping her down to the west'ard, whilst the strong wind was lying her over to the east'ard; a state of affairs which, owing to the increasingly choppy sea and the resulting heavy spray, quickly disposed of any coal dust that may have been left in any non-accessible place in any part of the deck, or anywhere ten feet above. The dark green of Woodspring hill could clearly be seen right ahead.

The mate, seeing the anxious glances Captain Trumper was casting aloft, told Arthur to cast off the coils of the topsail halyards and stand by ready to run the sail down if given the word. They were now well in over the English grounds and George could see the ridge of the Langford sands, the tail of which they would soon have to pass. He was on familiar ground now and, as he expected, he could see the highest part of the ridge was on the western end. This, as he pointed out to the Captain, was the result of such a long spell of easterly winds which they had experienced on the dreary passage over from the Irish coast.

'Captain', said George—for he noticed the worried look on the Captain's face—'With this strong breeze we can afford to keep down clear of the tail of the sand altogether and take her in to within a cable's length of the St Thomas's Head. The ebb's a bit strong in there but with the topsail she'll run up over that.' Then he added, 'If she don't stem it, there's plenty of water astern of her in there!'

Arthur, looking out of his galley doorway on the windward side—where he was only two steps from the topsail halyards—called out to say he could see sheep on the hill. It was a huge flock, weaving about like an enormous white blanket, obviously being rounded up by a dog.

Now they could see the dog: 'Time you took over I think George', said the Captain, indicating the wheel. The mate found it needed all his weight to keep the ship from luffing up, but this was good, he knew she'd stem the little tide race they would encounter when rounding St Thomas's Head. Exhilarated at the thoughts of entering the old and isolated river he knew so well, in addition to the satisfaction of being proved right in his advice to the Captain, he called to Arthur to stand by to ease off the main sheet. Looking straight at Captain Trumper he said, 'Shall I stand by the mizzen sheet, Captain?' The Captain, scenting George's dilemma, that it may be imprudent to give an order to himself, said 'You stay where you are George, and don't be afraid to holler!'

The mate watching the changing scene ashore as the tide swept them to the westward, and glancing astern every few seconds where he could see the N.W. Elbow Buoy, was waiting until St Thomas's Head, the ship, and the buoy were in one straight line, for then he knew they would be below the extreme tail of the Langford Grounds.

There they were, dead in line! 'Ease off the sheets main and mizzen!', he called. A few seconds was all that was needed for that very simple operation

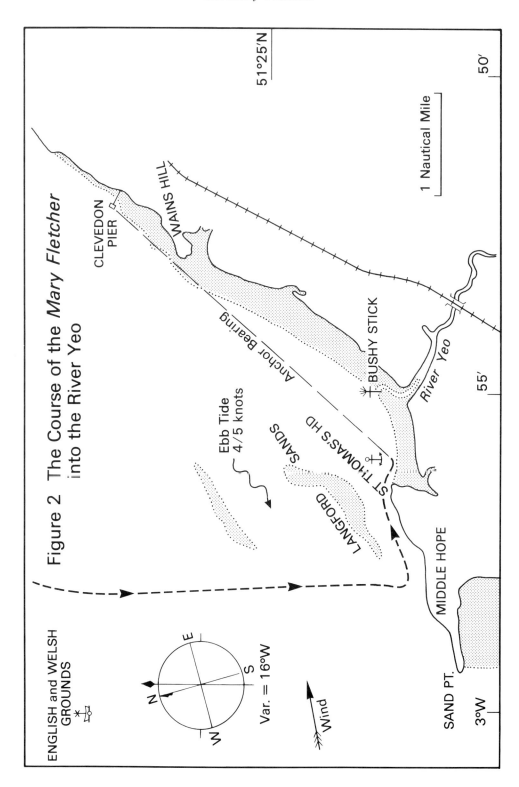

Figure 2 The Course of the *Mary Fletcher* into the River Yeo

Plate 36 *Palace*
'With Clevedon Pier open just clear of Wains Hill.' The trow *Palace*, built at Brimscombe, Gloucestershire, in 1827, discharging stone for repairing the sea walls at the mouth of the River Yeo in 1934. Wains Hill and Clevedon Parish Church are visible in the background across the levels. Grahame Farr

(getting them in was the problem). The vessel was now just above the Middle Hope Cove, not much more than half a cable from the rocky shore and, with the wind dead astern the strain on the helm had eased.

With the current running out at about 4 to 5 knots, just at that spot the *Mary Fletcher* was only doing some two knots over the ground. Without the topsail she would never have made it to the anchorage. But only about a mile to go, and still nearly two hours to low water. Rounding the head, George edged her in out of the tide race; called to Arthur to run the topsail down and was amused to see Captain Trumper run forward to give the cook a hand. Under the lee of the hill the wind lost its force. With Clevedon Pier open just clear of Wains Hill (Plate 36) the mate called 'Run down the jibs' and, as the sails came rasping down the stays he put the helm down and rounded the *Mary Fletcher*'s head to wind. The Captain let go the staysail halyard, George called to Arthur to let go the anchor as soon as he saw the ship was making sufficient stern way. Eighteen hours after starting to load in the Newport River the *Mary Fletcher* was quietly at

anchor with her 130 tons of cargo near the mouth of the River Yeo (Plate 37), and during that time the crew had managed a fair night's sleep.

The Captain, walking aft where George was lowering the peak of the mizzen said, 'You handled her well George, very well. You saved us a tide too!' 'Done it quite a few times in the old *Sarah*', said George, 'No hope though with the wind easterly. We might be able to get her up to the pier tonight if its not overcast, there's nearly a full moon.' George noticed the Captain looking to the eastward obviously trying to locate the river's mouth. But the River Yeo peters out as it flows on the wide expanse of the mud flats and from seaward can only be picked out at highwater.

Training the binoculars to where he knew the river was he was glad to see the 'bushy stick' was still standing where he and his father had stuck it in about five years before on the lowest part of the bar, about three quarters of a mile away.

All this was pointed out to Captain Trumper, who was quick to realise that the only way a stranger could find the mouth of the Yeo from seaward would be to wait for high water when the course of the river could be seen between the saltings. A welcome call from Arthur to say dinner was ready reminded them they had not eaten, or even had a cup of tea, since they were dropping down the River Usk.

Whilst enjoying that meal, they felt the vessel tilt a little. It was now nearing low water and the *Mary Fletcher* had touched the ground. 'Nothing to worry about', George said 'the bed of the "gut" shifts its course in accordance with the movement of the Langford Grounds after a long spell of Easterly or Westerly winds. But the channel around the Head itself is always there,' he added. After dinner, when the mate had made sure that the lead of the anchor chain was such that the ship, when the flood returned, would swing clear of her anchor, the crew turned into their bunks with the alarm in the cabin set for four o'clock.

Rested and refreshed, at that hour the Captain and George set the mizzen whilst Arthur brewed the inevitable mugs of tea. George's plan was simple; the wind was still fresh and westerly, and he estimated there would still be enough daylight left by the time there was sufficient water over the bar, for out of the flats in twilight the muddy water of the incoming tide would be the same colour as the mud itself. Only the bushy sapling would be the real guide.

With the anchor hove up just clear of the water (Plate 38), the standing jib was set, George took the helm and with a favourable wind and tide, the *Mary Fletcher* stood up towards the mouth of the Yeo. Although Arthur was stationed in the bows to look out for the 'bushy stick' it was the mate who, knowing where to look, saw it first.

Left Plate 37 *Clara May* at anchor
'Eighteen hours after starting to load in the Newport River the *Mary Fletcher* was quietly at anchor with her 130 tons of cargo near the mouth of the River Yeo . . ..' The ketch *Clara May* at anchor, waiting for the tide to go to a berth up a Devon river. Note the Board of Trade loadline or 'Plimsoll mark'. Basil Greenhill

The Captain, at the mate's suggestion, stood by the jib halyard ready to let it go when George gave the word, and Arthur stood by the down-haul ready to haul the sail down.

That particular evening the sunset and moonrise fortunately coincided to within a few minutes. Only about a cable's length to go now. The mate had warned Captain Trumper they were a bit early, and that the vessel may well 'smell the ground' as they crossed the bar, 'But we've got no speed Cap'n with this bit of sail, and if we touch its all soft mud!!'

The ship was nearly abreast of the marker now. All three men felt it, just a gentle lift of the decks under their feet, and a noticeable drag in the momentum of the ship but only for a couple of moments of time. Loaded as she was, with her own weight she just slid over. 'Down jib!', came the call from George, and in a few seconds it was down. The river there was less than half a cable wide, and a short 'kink' in its course thereabout made it necessary to luff the ship up nearly head to wind, but only for about two of her lengths, to keep her off the opposite bank. With the helm hard down and the mizzen boom hauled in by Captain Trumper, the old vessel, travelling only at a walking pace, did exactly as the mate hoped she would—forged ahead nearly head to wind, helped too by the stream, and reached the next bend

Calling to Arthur to hoist up the jib again, and asking the Captain to ease off the mizzen sheet, the *Mary Fletcher* with the wind abeam was now in the stretch of river between the saltings, (Plate 39) and it was still 1½ hours to high water. Meantime the moon, nearly full, was well above the horizon unobscured by any cloud. Captain Trumper, standing beside George said, 'That's not the first time you carried out that manoeuvre George. I would never have attempted it myself.' George replied, 'Neither would anybody else, without they were mad, not knowing what was under their bottom. As it happens there's nothing but soft mud.'

Less than half an hour brought them up to Pugs Pit, which is a little pill where the river bends and is wider than in most places. Here George called to Arthur to take down the jib, and at the same time he put the helm down and stuck the ship's bows into the weather bank. The tide and the wind in the mizzen swung her stern upstream.

Came the call to Arthur to lower the anchor down to the forefoot and, as soon as she floated clear, to give her about six fathom of chain. They were now within three cable's length of the discharging berth. In a few minutes the rising tide lifted the vessel's bow clear and, as she made stern way, her bow was sheered off to the centre of the river, the anchor let go and five or six fathom of cable paid out, not to bring the ship up, but enough to keep her head to the stream whilst dragging the anchor along the river's bed acted as a drogue. In a little over half

Left Plate 38 *Clara May*
'With the anchor hove up just clear of the water, the standing jib was set . . ..' The stem and the starboard bow of the ketch *Clara May* as she works, with the anchor just not clear of the water, upstream to a tidal berth. Basil Greenhill

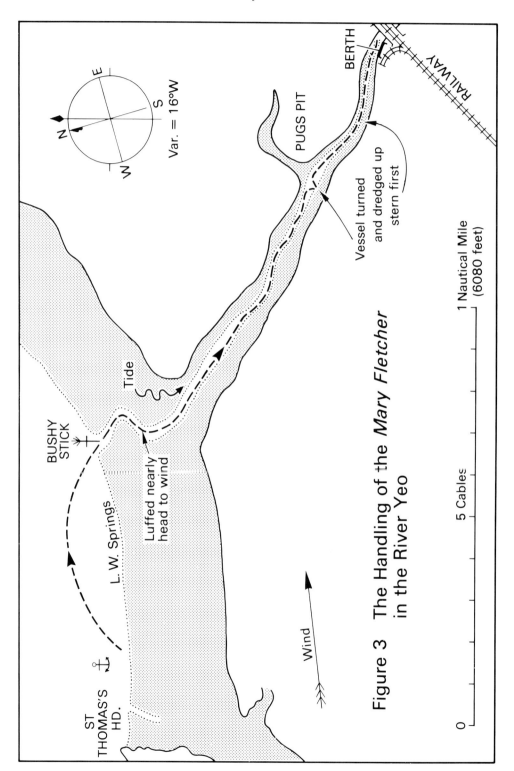

Figure 3   The Handling of the *Mary Fletcher* in the River Yeo

Plate 39   River Yeo
'The *Mary Fletcher* with the wind abeam was now in the stretch of river between the saltings . . ..' In
this photograph of this stretch of the River Yeo, the saltings are just being covered by the rising tide.
Basil Greenhill

an hour they were abreast of the Weston, Clevedon and Portishead Light
Railway's wharf beside the river. Leaving the anchor off in the river, the mate
sheered the vessel in, whilst Arthur paid out the chain cable.

The *Mary Fletcher* came to rest beside the piles with the slightest of bumps.
They had now only to moor her with plenty of 'drift' to the bow and stern ropes
and all was well.

Not being yet high water and the *Mary Fletcher* loaded deep as she was, the sea
banks on either side of the river were higher than eye level to the crew on the
deck (Plate 40). Captain Trumper looked around at the moonlit scene with
wonder in his eyes.

'Don't anybody live hereabouts George?', asked the Captain. Pointing to the
upright ladder fixed to the piles George replied: 'If you'll go up the ladder you'll
see all the lights that are here to see. All the land for miles around is below sea
level by nearly ten feet.'

The nearest light the Captain could see from the deck of the pier was about a
quarter of a mile away. It was the window of a farmhouse. As far as the eye
could see on either side were the lights of dwellings; few and far between. A
blaze of lights to the north east was the town of Clevedon, and to the south west
some miles away the lights of Worlebury hill. It made him feel the spot to which
he had brought the *Mary Fletcher* was the loneliest place on earth.

Arthur, coming aft to George and taking advantage of the Captain's absence on the pier said: 'Blimee George! No wonder you'm a wild man!! I never seed a place as dreary as this—not even in Ireland.'

The next morning the swiftly rising tide in the River Yeo lifted the *Mary Fletcher* high enough to allow her Master—after swinging himself up on to the gallant rail, by grasping the mizzen shrouds, and then pulling himself up from the gallant rail to the mizzen rigging sheerpole where he could stand in comfort—to look over the sea banks and, it being full daylight at high water, to have a panoramic view of the surrounding countryside. Captain Trumper could hardly believe his eyes, he felt he was looking down into a mighty arena, not an arena of combat, but an arena where cattle grazed and people lived below sea level. He saw a man ploughing a field with two horses pulling the plough and, in the distance a dog rounding up some sheep. The high tide, now within three feet of the top of the sea bank—the wavelets on the now wide waters of the river dancing red with the reflection of the crimson disk of the sun, now showing above the Clevedon hills—seemed to the Captain to be such a menacing and mighty force, held in check only by man made earthenbanks, that he wondered how folks could trust their lives in such precarious surroundings. Yet, he mused, he could see churches and plenty of tall elm trees, evidence enough that the danger was minimal.

'Having a look around Cap'n?', said a voice behind him. It was George the mate, just out of his bunk. He had set his alarm clock for 8 a.m. for that was the time the first passenger train would be due from Clevedon on her first journey to Weston Super Mare. If the ship broker at Newport had telephoned the Railway Company to tell them the *Mary Fletcher* had sailed the day before, as promised, probably the crane driver would arrive on the train. 'George', said Captain Trumper, 'It's a wonder the people can sleep in peace when the tides are as high as this!' 'Get away', said George, 'The tide's only really high for an hour or so, even spring tides like this one now. Nobody ever thinks about it. But the banks did break once, and there's a water mark all around the walls of the church, inside, showing how high the water rose, but that was over three hundred years ago in 16.. something!'

George, standing on the gallant rail, was pointing out to the Captain the house where he was born and where the family now lived right near the foreshore, when they heard the shrill whistle of the engine pulling the train from Clevedon. 'Here she comes', said George, 'That's the old *Hesperus;* she was old when I was a toddler, always wheezing!!' 'Only three carriages?', said the

Left Plate 40   *Jane*
A few pieces of broken concrete are now all that remains of the wharf at which the *Mary Fletcher* discharged on the River Yeo in Somerset, but this photograph of the ketch *Jane*, built at Runcorn in 1800, lying at Uphill Quay on the Axe a few miles to the west of the Yeo, shows a vessel in a very similar position to the *Mary Fletcher* after she had been brought up to the wharf and the tide had ebbed, leaving her deck well below the sea banks on either side. Note the staysail boom and the topsail stowed aloft. Edmund Eglinton

Captain. 'Why! they've got braking platforms like the carriages in America!' As the little train came puffing up the gentle slope that was necessary to carry the track over the sea banks, the driver kept up a series of blasts on the whistle. This the mate explained to the Captain was the welcome that was always given to a vessel that arrived, for in that very lonely spot on the River Yeo, the arrival of a ship was a great occasion.

Yes the train was slowing down, the guard could be seen on the braking platform applying the carriage brakes by screwing down the wheel on the breaking column. A second man appeared on the platform. The mate recognised him immediately, it was the crane drive Jack Payne.

The *Mary Fletcher,* less than a hundred yards from the little train, must have looked a pretty sight, for she was a very well kept and beautiful vessel and, floating as she was high above the surrounding countryside, her rigging and cordage lit by the slanting rays of the morning sun, a vision of loveliness.

The crane driver—he was actually one of the locomotive drivers—had known George Cox since early boyhood. They had grown up together. Their derisive remarks and banter towards each other were proof that they were friends of long standing. Actually, Jack Payne was doubly pleased to see his friend—who he had thought was still in the Railway Company's ketch *Sarah*—because of the eccentricity of the old steam crane. Even in those days, the 1920s, she was old and unreliable. When lifting a skip full of coal, jets of steam hissed out from every joint. Worse, the friction brake would not always hold when the skip was full.

The crews in the Railway Company's two vessels knew all about the crane and, when shovelling out the coal in the hold were always wary, and ready to jump clear when a shout came from above. Jack Payne had been threatened with a beating up on one or two occasions by strange crews when a loaded skip, owing to a fall in steam pressure and the faulty brake came slowly, but very frighteningly, back down into the hold. He was more than glad therefore that the mate of the strange vessel was George Cox, who would make his shipmates aware of all the troubles.

The crew of the *Mary Fletcher* had no thought of their ship being a 'vision of loveliness' on that sunny November morning. There was no romance in the knowledge that 130 tons of coal had to be shovelled out of the ship in well under twenty hours with only the mate and the able seaman using the No. 10 shovels. The skipper would be the man in the railway truck, his job being to knock out the catch on the iron skip holding about twelve hundred weights of coal as the skip came swinging and gyrating over the truck. Not a job to be envied, for the tipper had not only to be watchful, but extremely agile. Should the crane be swung around too speedily on its base, it could not always be stopped in time, causing the tipper to jump for his life.

Nevertheless the crew had ample time to uncover the hatchways as the *Mary Fletcher* sank down into the river on the swiftly ebbing tide. It would take Jack

Payne two hours to top the water up in the boiler of the crane, get the fire going, and raise a full head of steam. The hold of the vessel was about ten feet deep, and for the two shovellers digging down through that depth of coal and filling the skip to the brim time after time was the hardest graft of all (Plate 41). The large lumps were the biggest nuisance, too big to be handled even by a No. 10 shovel, they had to be pulled out by hand and lifted into the skip. Yet before the halt for the midday meal was called, the ceiling (floor) of the hold had been exposed on both sides of the massive keelson (Plate 42). Not so much shovelling to do now for the skip could be tilted into the face of the coal, a 'run' could be started from the near upright face half filling the skip without any shovelling. Thus two skilful men were able to get 130 tons of coal out of a vessel's hold in fifteen hours or even less.

The total freightage for bringing that cargo from Newport to the River Yeo and discharging it was, at that time £13.10s.10d. in old money, (or £13.60p) one third of that stupendous sum of money, £4.10.3d. would go to the owners; the same amount for the expenses of the ship herself, the remaining £4.10s.3d. for the wages of the Captain and crew (but it must be remembered that Captain Trumper had shares in the vessel and so he was paid twice).

Back again to the graft and black dust of discharging. By noon the next day thirteen ten-ton railway truck loads had been discharged in time for Captain

Plate 41   Discharging
'The hold of the vessel was about ten feet deep, and for the two shovellers digging down through that depth of coal and filling the skip to the brim time after time was the hardest graft of all.' Discharging a vessel with a skip and steam crane. Basil Greenhill

Plate 42   Hold of the *Hobah*
'Yet before the halt for the midday meal was called, the ceiling (floor) of the hold had been exposed on both sides of the massive keelson.' The hold of the ketch *Hobah*, showing the keelson with its protecting iron straps, the heel of the mainmast and the iron hanging knees. Basil Greenhill

Trumper to board the train to Clevedon and collect his hard-earned freight whilst the crew put on the hatches and swept the decks, thus making all ready to wash the ship down as soon as the evening tide came around her.

It was late afternoon before the flowing tide came lapping around the bilges of the *Mary Fletcher*. The two men, anxious as they were to go below and get the aggravating coal dust off their persons, and especially out of their hair, stuck to the general rule and proceeded to wash down the decks before opening up the companionways to the cabin and forecastle, thus preventing the black powder-like dust being wafted below by even the tiniest air of wind.

The water had to be drawn up over the side by a bucket attached to a lanyard. With the water at bilge strake level this meant a fifteen feet haul up to lift the bucket clear of the bulwarks. Although the draw bucket only held about a gallon and a half it was hard graft hauling up at least four a minute. There was much skill in that seemingly simple operation; the bucket had to fall 'mouth down' yet at a slight angle so as not to trap the air and then a quick flip to bring the bucket clear of the water, then about three or four quick jerks hand over hand upwards, and it was swung over the bulwarks with hardly any spillage. As the water was heaved along the deck—and especially in the angles of the bulwarks and stanchions, the man with the deck broom scrubbed away furiously, for in spite of the buckets of water heaved with speed and precision by the mate the oily dust would not be swilled away without the assistance of the broom.

The two men were having their 'bucket baths', the mate in his room and Arthur in the forecastle, when Captain Trumper returned by the 7 o'clock train from Clevedon. The Captain had brought fresh bread. After such a day Arthur could hardly be expected to provide a cooked supper. Instead, he had put half a dozen huge Irish potatoes in the galley oven to bake in their jackets and these, with cold boiled ham, which was usually kept for such occasions together with pickles, made a 'tea come supper' that really hungry men could appreciate and enjoy to the full.

When Arthur left the cabin with the crockery to wash up in the galley, the Captain, looking hard at the mate, said 'I know we're only just over a mile from the mouth of the river George, but any wind from West to North would pen us in here; couldn't even dredge down under the anchor against anything that was near a fresh breeze, but there you know that better than I do!'

George, well aware of what Captain Trumper had in mind replied: 'I was going to suggest Cap'n that we drop down the river tonight. The moon'll soon be up, and as soon as the tide eases we could get her off to midstream, let go the anchor, and drop her down to the mouth of the river. We were trapped up here once or twice when I was in the *Sarah.*'

Captain Trumper, with a look of relief on his face, said 'Thanks, George. You two fellows have had two days on the shovels. I didn't think it fair to ask you to take on so much anchor drill before you both got some sleep.' He added 'I feel all in myself anyway—after dodging that swinging skip for two days!'

Footsteps were heard on the deck above. It was Arthur wanting to know where he could get some cigarettes—'like been in the wilderness' he said. 'Come on down here!', said the mate. When Arthur appeared, looking a bit suspicious, the mate continued, 'Tis a wilderness Art'! more than two miles to the nearest shop, or pub. That means four miles there and back!'

The Captain, pulling open a drawer, one of many that matched in colour and shape the curved teak panelling of the cabin, took out a packet of twenty Players and handing them to Arthur said: 'Have these on the ship Arthur. We're leaving here at high water. Can't miss this lovely fine night. Plenty of time to sleep once we're clear of the mouth—that's what George says!—and he'll have to be the pilot tonight.' Arthur, smiling at the Captain, and thanking him for the precious cigarettes, turned an accusing eye on the mate saying: 'You told me today you would be going home to see your parents tonight George!' George replied 'There was a fresh wind up the river then. Can't miss a flat calm and this lovely moonlight, may be trapped in here for days. No shops, no pubs, no girls, then who'd holler the loudest—you! you silly gert bugger!'

Arthur, offering the mate a cigarette, from the new packet said 'Have one of my fags Pilot!!' There was no animosity between those two fellows. Friction between two men in such circumstances would have made life quite intolerable. Working a heavy vessel like the *Mary Fletcher* with just the master and two crew was a never-ending grind of unbelievingly hard, but skilful, work. In bad weather at sea the lack of sleep, and man power to handle the heavy booms and flogging sails as the ship went about whilst beating to windward made the work extremely dangerous and exhausting. Yet men such as the crew in the *Mary Fletcher* whose families had manned those little ships for generations stayed on. They had no alternative. They had no means of raising the capital to buy modern tonnage. More and more of the ketches were being fitted with slow running semi-diesel auxiliary engines which effectively made them motor-sailers. Two years later the *Mary Fletcher* herself was to have one. With the help of the engines and motor winches it was going to prove possible to grind a hard living out of the ketch for another generation until the 1950s.

As the tide eased, nearing high water, the crew took in the four inch bow and stern ropes, but not before two small lines had been passed around convenient piles forward and aft to act as slip ropes. With the last few minutes of the tide the forward slip rope was taken in—for the ship's bow was pointing down-stream—the vessel's bow hauled off to the anchor using the windlass. The *Mary Fletcher,* empty of cargo or ballast, would have had a displacement of over a hundred tons, yet in dead calm weather and no current to reckon with at slack water it was amazing how easily such a ship seventy-five feet long could be moved.

The Captain walked forward to where the mate and Arthur, having broken out the anchor, were slacking away the anchor chain to lower the 10cwt anchor so that the crown just touched the bed of the river. This would stop her way with no danger of the chain fouling the stock. Immediately the ebb started giving the ship a little stern way more chain would be slacked away, thus allowing the stock to lie on the bottom and ensuring the fluke would 'dig' itself into the blue clay of the river's bed.

The ship would now have to be steered as she dropped astern with the tidal stream. For every bend in the course of a river there is usually a bank of mud or sand jutting out one side, and a steep-to bank on the opposite side. However, there are never two the same, and that is why local knowledge is necessary, and why Captain Trumper had said George the mate would have to be the pilot (Plate 43), for should the vessel's stern touch a shoal point, her bow might swing across the stream and touch the opposite shore—with disastrous results on the ebb tide. Before anything could be done to get her free, the falling tide would quickly cause the hull to be severely strained at the very least, but more than likely her back would be completely broken.

The mate had been watching the lights ashore, for they now had an extensive view over the sea banks. 'We've just started to drop astern Cap'n', said George. 'Get back and get hold of the wheel then George' replied the Captain, 'Don't

Right Plate 43   Sketch Chart
Masters of vessels trading occasionally into tidal rivers like the Yeo used sometimes to make their own rough sketch charts. Here is one made by Captain Alexander Murdoch, owner and master of the ketch *Garlandstone*, showing the approach to a quay on an Irish River. Michael Leszczynski

very
close
together

railings —

railings

end of 2nd ... Bridge

railings & fences

... better corner of
... high railings
... low arch

there is a high

2nd ...

forget we draw nearly six feet light. Arthur and I will manage the anchor drill. Don't be afraid to holler for more chain!'

A vessel dropping astern on a tidal stream had never to be allowed to travel as fast as the tidal stream, otherwise the rudder had no power to sheer the ship away from any hazard known to be in, or close to the fairway. Obscure rivers were not buoyed, local knowledge therefore was essential.

Dropping past Pugs Pit bend, an eddy swung the vessel's stern uncomfortably near the point, in spite of the helm being hard over.

'Give her some chain Cap'n', called the mate. 'Four or five fathom, bring her up!'

He could hear them furiously paying out the heavy chain—the links forged out of 7/8″ iron rod—this pulled the anchor deep into the mud, bringing the ship to a standstill. George Cox could hear the roar of the water as the swift current tore past the nearly half exposed rudder.

In less than a minute the vessel was out into mid-stream, the anchor leading straight ahead. 'Have in some chain!' called the mate: 'Start her off again. We're past the worst bit Cap'n!' The clank, clank, clank, of the four massive pawls of the windlass, on that very lovely and peaceful moonlit night as the chain came in started up the flocks of wild duck and widgeon from their feeding on the waters edge; and these in turn 'called up' the pee-wits from their sleeping quarters in the rough grasses on the shore side of the sea bank.

'Pay out a fathom or so Cap'n she's not answering too well!' And so it went on down that lonely mile of river. The tide running out at about 2½ knots an hour meant that the ship, owing to the necessity of dropping astern at only half the speed of the stream, and with the few times she was completely stopped for a minute or two, took a full hour to reach the river's mouth.

It must be mentioned here, that when a ship was being dredged up a river with her anchor down, there was little, if anything, for the master to worry about. Should the vessel touch a shoal, or a bank of the river, the rising tide would quickly set her free. (No ship could ever be dredged up a river which had any rock in its bed).

A cable's length (200 yards) out from the foreshore the vessel was brought up with fifteen fathom of chain, for at that distance off the flow of the ebb from the river was useless, the now swiftly flowing ebb was sweeping down the flats, crossing the river at right angles. When the flats ebbed up the ship would still be in the river. Should the wind come in, making it a lee shore, the ship could be easily dropped back into the river to a safe anchorage on the first of the flood tide. George Cox the mate had indeed proved himself by bringing the *Mary Fletcher* safely into the river, and by getting her safely out with no wind.

NOTES ON 'DREDGING' AND OTHER METHODS OF MOVING A VESSEL IN A TIDAL RIVER

The practice of moving a vessel in a tideway by the use of her anchor as described in the passage up the rivers Usk and Yeo, is still used today on the River Tamar. The restored local barge *Shamrock* is ketch rigged as she was in 1899, and does not have an engine. Because she is rigged with masts and sails it is commonly presumed that the wind will supply the motive force. However, in a steep-sided valley with many twists and turns, this source of energy is fickle and unreliable. Furthermore, as the river narrows upstream the room for manoeuvre under sail is curtailed, making tacking impossible. This combination of sudden wind shifts and gusts without warning and a river which at times is not much wider than the vessel's length requires methods other than sailing to reach the destination.

The regular cycle of flood and ebb is far more predictable and is therefore, by comparison, a better source of motive power to harness than the wind. Due allowance must be made after periods of heavy rain as the river flow, especially as a vessel goes upstream, can override the expected flood tide to such an extent as to cancel it out, although the level will still rise and fall, high water being in this sense greater than the tide tables predict.

For 'dredging' up, stern first to be effective, a good flow is required, a current of at least 2½ knots being about the minimum. Therefore it is not practical at neaps, or when trying to proceed upstream after heavy rain with all the fresh water coming down. Normally at spring tides the rate is sufficient with the biggest ranges giving 4 knots. Between the two extremes it may only be practical for an hour either side of half flood, although the ebb can be worked for a longer period.

Two things are important when dragging an anchor along the bottom. First, the nature of the river bed which is best if mud or clay; rocky and uneven bottoms with hidden snags are to be avoided. Secondly, the river is never of constant depth but usually deeper on the outside of the bends. This can lead to a lot of 'anchor work' as the 'hook' may no longer be in contact with the river bed in these deeper parts resulting in the vessel travelling at the same speed as the current with no flow past the rudder and hence not under control. By slacking away more cable she will once more be under command but on reaching a shallower stretch, this will be found to be too much, the vessel coming to a standstill. To get round this problem, we have found when working *Shamrock* that a plain length of chain (25 feet of ¾″ stud link) with a 2½″ manila line bent on is more effective. The vessel then will not come fast and should she be in danger of striking the banks and therefore has to be stopped quickly, the bow anchor can be let go. This length and size of drag chain suits *Shamrock* which is always on a light draught. Should she be loaded, extra chain would be required with perhaps a shaped weight on the end. Much depends on the size and displacement of the vessel and the strength of the current.

'Dredging' is best used on the flood tide when the depths are increasing, for should she run aground it will not be long before she floats clear. When used on the ebb, great care is needed, for she may get jammed across the river and with little or no support in the middle at low water her back could be broken. Therefore, local knowledge is essential.

Although this method is relatively safe and perhaps the only one available in prevailing circumstances, it does suffer from a few disadvantages. First, because the vessel is slowed down in relation to the free flow of the current, she will take longer to reach her destination than by just drifting along; some control can be provided by the ship's boat towing from ahead and in the case of barges, the use of poles and sweeps. Secondly, the rudder is very vulnerable if she touches the bottom, as in most cases it will be the first part to come in contact, the whole weight of the vessel being stopped suddenly by the blade which usually swings hard over one way or the other. Thirdly, should a breeze spring up and the direction be fair for sailing, the vessel is pointing the wrong way.

Figure 4 Dredging

The vessel in position (a) is drifting up with the tide, travelling at 4 knots over the ground, at the same speed as the current. However, there is no flow past the rudder which is therefore ineffective. The anchor is let go and sufficient cable veered to stop her. She will then swing head to stream (b). To make further progress under control, the rudder is put hard over to starboard, the vessel's stern cants to port and the cable is shortened in sufficiently for her to move over the ground once more, but at a reduced rate compared with the tidal flow. She will now drag the anchor, lying at an angle to the stream, moving stern first but bodily sideways as shown with the dotted lines. Assuming that there is no wind, if she is slowed to 2 knots over the ground, then a 2 knot flow is established past the hull and rudder and she will progress towards the right-hand bank of the river (c). Once clear of the obstruction in position (d) the rudder can be put amidships and she will continue to dredge up river in a straight line.

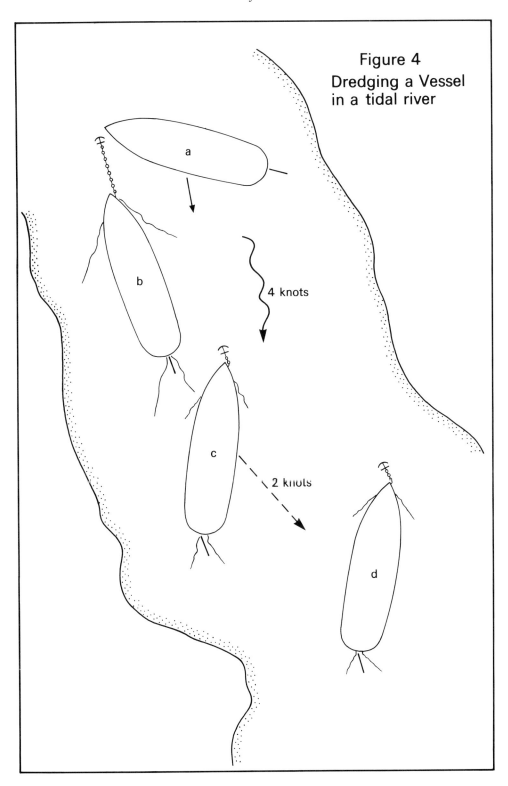

Figure 4
Dredging a Vessel
in a tidal river

4 knots

2 knots

It is often the case that the wind tends to blow 'up' or 'down' the river irrespective of its true direction, caused by the high steep banks. In the situation of a vessel using the flood tide to proceed up river and faced with a light breeze from the opposite direction, the river being too narrow to tack, the vessel may proceed up stern first under bare poles. Instead of a drag chain to slow her down, the wind will have the same effect and thus a flow is established past the rudder as she tends to blow back over the tide. Much depends on the relative strengths of the two opposing forces, wind and tide, and the vessel's draught, displacement and rig. Deep loaded, and hence with minimum windage of hull, mast and spars, some sail may be set, even the head of the staysail half-way up the stay can be enough. The object is to establish control without retarding progress too much as she moves up stern first with the tide. Even if the wind is blowing diagonally across the stream at a fine angle it should be possible to keep the vessel up to the weather bank.

Sometimes the breeze freshens to such an extent that it cancels out the tide even under 'bare poles', the vessel in this instance having a flow past the rudder equal to the strength of the current. She is under good control but can only sheer from side to side making no progress. With *Shamrock* we often use the ship's boat to lay out a kedge from the stern and haul her to windward. (Ketches tend to lie better with their bows downwind). The work required is not too stenuous as the anchor is carried out down tide all the time. Furthermore, should the breeze die down a bit once she is in the lee of a high bank, this kedging can be stopped and the vessel proceed as before.

Near the high water when the river is virtually at a 'stand' for an hour or so, should there be no wind *Shamrock* is often towed from ahead by the ship's boat, the line being made fast to the end of the bowsprit of the vessel and round the after thwart of the boat, to give her steering control and maximum leverage in turning the vessel, further help being provided by two sweeps.

In the same situation the barges that worked the upper reaches of the Tamar were often hauled up from a towpath on the bank, the line made fast to the mainmast in the form of a large bowline which was hoisted up as far as the shrouds allowed using one of the headsail halyards. This kept the tow clear of the reeds lining the river bank and also the pull was transmitted close to the pivot point of the vessel. If taken directly from the bow, unless the lead ahead was very long indeed, she would tend to turn into the bank, the rudder not being effective, at these very low speeds with no river flow, in keeping her off.

Poles are also handy for keeping *Shamrock* clear of the bank and overhanging trees and are a practical way of moving her near low water when the depths are least. At high water springs it is 15 to 18 feet deep in places and thus a very long pole indeed would be required. Our 16 foot long boat hooks which we find light and easy to use, are then ineffective.

Peter Allington

FURTHER READING

A number of books published in recent years have put on record a great deal of the background to the sort of seafaring activity which is described in such detail in the *Mary Fletcher*. Among them are:

E. Eglinton, *The Last of the Sailing Coasters*, London, 1982.

W. J. Slade, *Out of Appledore*, London, 1980.

W. J. Slade and B. Greenhill, *Westcountry Coasting Ketches*, London, 1974.

E. Hughes and A. Eames, *Portmadog Ships*, Caernarfon, 1975.

A. Eames, *Ships and Seamen of Anglesey*, Llangefni, 1973.

G. Farr, *Somerset Harbours*, London, 1954.

G. Farr, *Ships and Harbours of Exmoor*, 1974.

M. Bouquet, *No Gallant Ship*, London, 1959.

B. Shaw, *Schooner Captain*, Truro, 1972.

T. Coppack, *A Lifetime with Ships*, Prescot, 1973.

C. H. Ward-Jackson, *Stephens of Fowey*, London, 1980.

C. H. Ward-Jackson, *Ships and Shipbuilders of a Westcountry Seaport. Fowey, 1796–1939*, Truro, 1986.

B. Norman, *Tales of Watchet-Harbour*, Watchet, 1985.

B. Greenhill, *The Merchant Schooners*, London, 1988.

B. Greenhill, *The Evolution of the Wooden Ship*, London, 1988.